HEY GEORGIA

Frederick Rook

ISBN: 9798366633635

Chapter 1

"Yeah, I heard you Bruno. You want to smooth out the grade on the left side of the roadway. That section needs more gravel underneath before you do that, though. And I know you know that too," he said. Mike Netherland was a senior road construction engineer. He held his cell phone to his ear, listening, nodding lightly while he did.

"I know it's a pain in the ass. But it'll be a lot worse for all of us, and that means you, if we have to repair a sunken roadway later," Mike said. On the other end of the line, Bruno, one of his construction superintendents, was explaining something to him when Mike noticed a woman walk through the front door of the Super24. It was just after six thirty in the morning and already bright outside. It was getting warm out too. Netherland wasn't really a girl watcher, but he had a 'good eye' and followed her a moment as she walked towards the coffee bar, right near where he was standing. Mike turned a moment to look behind him; he was waiting for the Guatemala to finish brewing, which was empty when he came in a minute ago. As the project site manager, he was getting coffee for himself and his two construction supers. Something he did often. They were working on a stretch of new toll road on Highway 95, twenty minutes north of where he was currently standing. It was already late May, and they were two months behind. Kiewit, the construction company he worked for, had a sterling record of quality work. You paid for it, but you got your money's worth when you did. They still barely got the contract though, since they were always high. The problem for the state and the highway department, who were overseeing the work for the toll road, was all the best companies were busy on current jobs and tied up to far out in time. This was true for Kiewit too, but they had staffing available to fill the contract at normal pricing. That being high. Lower cost firms that were available had poor records; and this was a critical length of road. It was never a good idea to do sub par work anyway because it didn't 'save' any money long term. Kiewit knew they were worth what they charged and were world regarded for their knowledge and skill on roadways.

The woman poured herself a cup of hazelnut coffee, and while it flowed out of the pot's spout, she turned and looked at Mike. He averted his eyes, not even thinking that he'd been watching her.

"Netherland, are you there?"

"Yeah, I'm right here. I was checking to see if the coffee was ready yet," he said.

"Well, what do you think? About what I just said?"

"Run it by me again, Bruno. I got most of it, but what'd you say again?" he said.

"Mike, what's up? I just explained—"

"Don't break my balls, Bruno; I'm trying to get some coffee here for us. Just run it by me again, all right?" he said.

"Sure. No problem Mike," he said. And went through his suggestion again that they consider using some of that new underlayment material instead of more gravel. It was a new Caterpillar product. One that'd be faster and easier to set it than as many dump trucks of gravel as they'd need.

"It's an approved substitute, Mike," Bruno said. Finishing the original suggestion.

"No, I don't want to use that because I don't trust it yet. It would be better to do it the 'hard way' and use the gravel. I know that works. We're already behind, so what's an extra day going to matter? Let some other construction company test out the Cat product first. I don't want to be the one that gets burned on an unproven product," he said.

She was adding cream and sugar to her coffee at the stand near the coffee pots. A trim brunette with short, dark brown hair; which suited her perfectly. She wore fashionable navy blue pants that weren't tight but fit her well, a light beige rayon blouse, and a narrow peach colored leather belt. Late forties, maybe fifty. Great posture too; someone that took care of herself. A subdued but definitely nice figure, along with everything else. When she finished stirring up her coffee, she snapped a lid on it and turned to face Mike. Right where she was standing. Her hands weren't on her hips literally, but that's what her body language showed. He lifted the edge of the cowboy hat he was wearing lightly. A gesture of courtesy. He'd taken it off when he first came in, but put it back on when Bruno called.

"Ok Bruno, I'll see you in a few minutes. I'm about to leave with our coffees," he said. He put the phone in his pocket and she stood looking at him.

"Can I help you?" he said. Mike realized now he'd been watching the woman the whole time and knew it wasn't polite. He couldn't undo it and his question was the best he could come up with at the moment.

"I'm wondering if there's something you needed from me? You were watching me the whole time, so I thought you must either know me or had a question," she said. Mike was embarrassed but also amused by how forward she was.

Always gentlemanly, Mike wanted to wrap this up as well as he could and scoot with the coffees.

"I'm terribly sorry, ma'am. I really am." Mike told her he was talking with one of his men and admitted he was absentmindedly looking at her.

"I should say so," she said. She turned to go to the register with her coffee but made an about face, set her coffee down on the mixing stand and looked at Mike.

"I'd love to know what you found so interesting, why you were looking at me," she said. Mike was filling his cups with coffee and wanted to get to the site. There was a lot to do today, and he needed to take advantage of the good weather when they had it.

"Look lady please, I shouldn't have stared. I'm sorry, I really am. I wasn't even thinking about what I was doing. It's very impolite, I know. How about I pay for your coffee and we call it a day—we can still be friends?" he said. She made a huff sound. It hadn't been a good morning for her, even before leaving her house, and she realized she was taking it out on this guy who looked at her. It wasn't the first time a man looked at her, but it hit her wrong today.

"We won't be friends, that's for certain. But I'll make a deal with you. I'll buy your coffee for you if you tell me what you were thinking," she said.

"I have to go lady, I'm sorry. What can I say?"

"I'll pay for all your three of those coffees if you'll tell me," she said. Mike couldn't believe what he'd gotten himself into. Already late to the site, and he knew he'd taken more than a quick glance, though he wasn't exactly gawking at her and definitely not 'undressing' her with his eyes.

"You're a nice unit for an old lady. That's what I was thinking, ok?" he said. His eyes were friendly, but he wanted to move on. Netherland didn't like loose ends, and he just blurted it out. It was the truth, and it seemed like she wouldn't leave him be if he didn't tell her.

"I didn't expect that," she said. Her expression softened a little. Not much, just a little.

"And I should give you a good slap for saying that, you know?" she said.

"You probably should," Mike said. There was a trace of a change in his facial muscles. Not even a shadow of a smile showed, but it was trying to.

"We're in public, so I'll leave it be," she said. She turned and headed to the register.

"So you're picking up the tab on these coffees?" he said.

"No," she answered.

"Ok, let me pay for yours then," he said.

"I got it," she said. She made the slightest wave with her free hand without looking behind her. Mike's facial muscles took a dive, and the biggest Cheshire grin in the world broke out on his face. You could almost 'hear' it. His phone rang in his pocket.

"Netherland," he said.

"You on your way yet to the site? We got a problem we need your help with. And I don't just mean we need our coffees, either." It was Bruno.

"Yep. On my way. Took a few minutes for them to brew our coffee. Headed out the door now," he said. Mike kept his eyes on the doorway and the woman never looked behind her after she paid. When she was at the door of her car, she took a sideways glance towards the entrance of the Super24.

"Old lady, my ass," she said under her breath. And got in her car and drove away.

Mike looked around when he came out of the store. He tried not to be conspicuous looking, but couldn't spot his 'new friend' anywhere.

"Just as well. That didn't go that great. She was a looker, though; especially for her age," he thought. He shook his head and laughed, considering the whole thing. Then hopped into his white Silverado and headed to the job site.

"What kept you?" Bruno said.

"Waiting for the coffee to brew and also a woman asked me a question," he said.

"I see. She ask you what time it was?" he said.

"Bruno I'm here. What's up?" he said. Bruno shook his head and looked at Mike. He'd replaced his cowboy hat with a Kiewit safety helmet. Bruno laid out the site construction diagram and showed him a possible drainage issue he wasn't sure they'd considered. He already called for the gravel and thought they might also need a runoff drain placed to the side of where the road would be. Mike looked at the site diagram and checked the survey numbers for pitch, then the expected water volume in a storm. He nodded and turned to another page in the package.

"Yeah. Good catch Bruno. Do we have a length of that here?"

"I wasn't certain we'd need it, which is why I asked you. I sent for it already. If you didn't think we'd need it, easier to cancel than to order it," he said.

"Right. Good work, man, real good. Here's your coffee. Where's Ray?" he said.

"In the tank, taking a leak. He'll be right out," Bruno said. Netherland was good-natured, but a force to be reckoned with as a construction engineer. Bruno was happy he'd been right about the possible drainage problem. He enjoyed working for Mike. The three of them made a strong road construction team. It ended up being one of those days where it seemed like they got a week's worth of work done in one long day.

Mike was driving south on Highway 95 heading towards home. They'd finished for the day, now already after seven.

"Good company and a good crew," he said to himself.

Exhausted after the full day. He blinked and realized how tired he felt.

"I've got to get a coffee and something to eat," he thought. He headed to an exit where he knew there was a Subway and a Starbucks close together. An idea struck him though, and he moved back into the thru lane and continued southward. Off the highway he pulled into the Super24 from this morning to get a coffee. After work, he usually went to the one further north for a Diet Coke and another coffee.

"A two-fisted drinker," he said. Grinning and shaking his head. "Probably too much caffeine. That's what Dolores always says." Dolores was Mike's sister. He got a cold Diet Coke and a cup of coffee. Regular was all they had fresh now. "Good enough," he thought. Unimpressed with the sandwich choices, he picked up a bag of jerky and some pickles from the refrigerated food section. He sat in the seat of his truck relaxing while he had his 'dinner.' He poured almost half the Coke down in a single long swallow. "Thirsty," he said. He looked around and shook his head. "What am I doing here?" he thought. Still thinking about the morning's interaction at the coffee bar.

"Crazy dame," he said. He got out of the truck and threw out the now empty jerky package, pickle bag and plastic soda bottle—taking the last gulp of what remained as he walked to the trash can.

"I'm closer to the house here anyway," he thought. He sat in his truck sipping the coffee. Set the half-full cup in the holder, started up and headed out.

"Time to go home," he said.

Chapter 2

Ray and Bruno were standing with Mike Netherland by the back of his pickup truck. The gate was down and Mike's cell phone was on speaker. It was a 'corporate meeting.' It was one reason the guys loved this kind of work. "Here's the job, get it done," was pretty much always the message. It was hard work, but low on bullshit. Perfect for people who worked hard, hated office politics, and in-person meetings. Kiewit didn't get to be the biggest private construction company in the United States by wasting time. They stood around the back of the truck together with their coffees in hand, and the corporate manager of the project was talking.

"What are you guys doing there? The road section is over five weeks behind schedule." It was Milton Cross. Head highway engineer at Kiewit corporate in Omaha.

"I know, I know. You think we don't know that, Milt?" Mike said. There are never any projects that don't have delays. There were always reasons, what's, and whys. Rain or snow, or a piece or two of large equipment that may have needed repair. Crew members and subs that were late or non performing. It was always something. They'd had some of each on this project. The real biggie was the weather—which cost them close to two weeks right off. That caused a problem with an equipment lease which needed to be extended. And so on and so forth.

"Milt, can you do anything for us about making sure we don't get any more rain?" It was Ray.

"Look guys, I'm not trying to break your balls. I was out there once, remember? But I've got to go through this and note everything. I got higher ups up my ass, and it's rolling down. But press hard on this. There's a contingency for two bigger sections further north up the road. We want that work. We're already there on the road and the boys here don't want that to slip through our hands," Milt said. Mike was nodding and looking at the guys. A 'let's finish up here so we can get back to work' expression on his face. Milton Cross was a good guy. They all knew he was once in the field. Most people who moved up at Kiewit were.

"Milt, no matter who did this, the job would've been delayed. The weather hit us hard. I think we've made up close to ten days the last week. It's been fabulous weather for a little while and things are coming together. We get everything you're saying, though. Why don't you let us get started here today," Mike said. It wasn't even seven, and they'd been at the site for over an hour already. After them, they had close to seventy men in various capacities working equipment, grading and hauling gravel. As well as doing other seemingly unrelated work that had a part in the final construction of the toll road.

It'd been two weeks since that early morning at the Super24. The 'crazy dame' a distant memory now. Another small chapter in life; the kind of thing that happens to all people, which eventually fades into the memory banks of our lives.

"Ray, while you're picking up the pipes we need at Gloucester's, get us a few coffees at the Super24 near the industrial park," Mike said.

"Mike, I can't right now unless you can wait over an hour.

I gotta go to my house before I come back. My wife's away and I have to pick up my son from school and bring him home. I'll bring some back after that," he said.

"Right, I forget. Don't worry about it. I'll go get `em. You want one too? Might be cold when you get back."

"Sure. That'd be great. I won't be more than an hour," Ray said. They worked fourteen-hour days most of the time, so Mike never sweated small life issues like this. Mike hopped in his truck and drove over to the Super24 up not too far from the stretch of road they were working.

"To the pump first," Mike said. The fuel gauge was low, and he wanted to fill up before going in for coffees. He tucked the receipt along with the company gas card in the small booklet in the glove compartment and was about to step out of the truck cab and his phone rang.

"Netherland," he said.

"Mike, it's Milt. I've got some good news for you," he said. And he told him about an aspect of the current section of road project which was being reduced in scope and would to save the company some time on the road section.

"Uh-huh. Wow, that's great Milt," he said. He was nodding and delighted to hear this. While he listened, Mike did a double take and saw out the window of his truck the same woman he'd run into a couple weeks ago at the Super24 closer to town. Mike thought she looked agitated.

"What's she doing up here?" he thought. Only half engaged listening to Milt's 'update' now. Mike was far enough away from the store at the pump, she couldn't see him. And the place was full of while Chevy and Ford work class pickup trucks getting gas. Unless you knew who you were looking for or at, you'd never be able to distinguish or notice anyone in particular. She was walking out of the store with a cup of coffee in her hand and a store bag with something in it. Mike was doing his best to stay focused on Milt's talking, giving him an appropriate 'uh-huh,' or 'that's good,' when it made sense. At the same time tried to see where the woman was going and unfortunately she blended in with several people walking around the side of the store to where there were a lot of cars and vehicles parked. They were coming and going so much it was impossible to see what car, SUV or whatever the woman or anyone else was driving.

Mike returned his full attention to Milt, asking for clarification on a point or two again. To get the complete story and end the call well. He wanted to make sure he understood the whole narrative correctly. When they'd hung up, he ventured into the store and got the coffees. What was curious when Mike had seen her walking out was her slow walk. Not like she was sick, but like something was weighing her down. He felt kind of bad now, laughing like he did that day, even though it was just to himself when he'd met her.

"Poor girl," he thought. He'd hoped to have been able to say 'hi' to her.

"Probably wouldn't've been a good idea, anyway. I don't think she likes me," adding to his thoughts. He took a good sized pull of his coffee. Replete with four packs of sugar and probably a quarter cup of light cream.

"Ahh, That's good," he said. He tipped his hat to a person who held the door open for him as he walked back out to his truck. Still at the pump he'd gotten gas from.

Ray was back at the site and the three of them, Mike, Ray, and Bruno, were looking at the construction drawings on the back of Mike's Silverado. There were some marked out pylons that were intended for setting high aluminum poles into for mounting electronic sensors. The company doing the electronic monitoring developed some devices that could be spaced further apart and they removed those from their job, which was the thing helping them make better time on the project the last few days. Following, the work progressed routinely for the day.

"You don't think they'll change their mind, do you Mike? It'll be a lot worse for us adding them back later, you know," Ray said. He was looking at the pylon structures on the drawings.

"I said the same thing to Milt. He said to proceed. If they change their mind later, it'll be a change order and they'd have to 'eat' the extra delay. I told him and he was certain," he said. Ray nodded, then shook his head. He'd been through similar 'approved' changes, which were 'final decisions.' And they still came back to bite them in the ass.

"Ok, what else right now?" Bruno said.

"That's it for now," Mike said. Folding up the papers and putting them back into the large polyethylene plan box. He turned to look and see how the heavy equipment operators were doing.

"These guys are good," Ray said. Looking at them while he stood by Mike. Mike nodded, then picked up his coffee from the back of the truck.

"Yeah, they are. It's about time we got some guys like this. Let's hope we can keep `em here until we're done with this stretch of road," he said.

"How'd you get my phone number? And why are you calling me, anyway?" she said.

"What's the matter—aren't you happy to hear from me?" the voice said on the other end of the line.

"Cam, what do you want? We're through, remember? Divorced and you're lucky you're not in prison," she said.

"That's not a very nice thing to say now, is it?" he said.

"How did you get this number, anyway? It's impossible," she said.

"Not for me, it's not. And what does it matter, anyway? I just wanted to call and say hello—and tell you how much I miss you," he said.

"Cam, please. Can't you just leave me alone?" she said. Tears formed in her eyes. From pain and fear. She heard him laughing quietly on the other end of the line. Furiously, she pressed the red 'end call' icon on her smart phone, ending the call. She looked at the side of the phone, then the other and the top. The phone rang again, and she pressed 'decline.'

"Here it is," she said. Clicking the phone 'airplane' mode button. She sat down on the porch at her sister's house, where she'd been standing when the call came. She sat on the colorful sunporch sofa and cried out loud. A deep, visceral cry, her body heaving with sobs. After a while, she tried to calm herself and wiped her eyes. She stood up, straightening up her clothes, then went into the house. In the bathroom, she washed her face, dried off and put the smallest amount of natural face powder on, then brushed her hair.

"I wonder if Phoebe'll notice," she thought.

"Her phone's off. That bastard found out her number. I guarantee it," Phoebe said. She'd tried twice and on the third time almost dropped her phone, because she pressed the 'end call' icon so hard. Phoebe was trying to call her sister and let her know she was running a little late. She'd picked up some sushi for the two of them for lunch. The place she was at was still making the bluefin tuna rolls, and she had to wait. Her tires almost squealed when she drove out of the shopping center to get home.

"I'd love to shoot the son of a bitch myself," Phoebe said to herself in the car. She didn't have a gun; just dreaming.

"Hey Sis, I'm back," Phoebe said. Gang busting into the house with their lunch and drinks.

"Hi Phoebe," she said.

"Fresh powder?' Phoebe said. Her sister laughed. Phoebe didn't miss much.

"I wanted a touch up," she said. Phoebe set the bag on the table and looked at her sister.

"He got your number and called you. I'm right, aren't I?"

she said. She loved her sister, and it sickened her that that menace was still alive and out there. Phoebe stood looking at her. Probably the one and only person she'd be glad to die for, especially if she could kill her sister's ex-husband in the process. Phoebe was the younger of the two of them. Always a pepperbox but a heart the size of the titanic. Phoebe held out her arms and when she did, her sister couldn't hold it in anymore and started sobbing. Phoebe held her, letting her cry. After a spell, she let her go and looked at her.

"Let's eat. I'd love to go kill him first, but since he's a 'ghost' and we're not going to find him, we should eat. You had nothing this morning and I'm starving," she said. Her sister wiped her eyes, and they sat down at the table.

"Here's your drink. Diet Dr. Pepper for you and a Sprite for me."

"Bluefin tuna rolls, Phoebe—where'd you get these?"

"Nothing's too good for you, woman. I know a place. They don't always have it; bluefin tuna, that is. I checked yesterday, and they said they'd have some today." They ate silently for a little while. Phoebe could see her sister was still. Her way of dealing with agitation—and fear. Phoebe realized no matter how much she wished Cam was dead, he wasn't. And talking too much about him did nothing to help her sister feel any happier. The lunch was bitter. It was great food, fabulously made. But it may as well've been rolls of cardboard right now. They took their time eating and not chatting a lot. Phoebe packed up the uneaten fish rolls for later.

"Thanks Phoebe. They were great. They really were. It's special—the bluefin tuna," she said.

"I'll put these away for later or tomorrow. Help yourself anytime, ok?" Phoebe said.

"Phoebe, I'm going back out onto the sun porch, if you don't mind. To watch and listen to the birds," she said.

"Go ahead Sis. You want a tea or coffee?" Phoebe said.

"That would be nice. Tea. You still have any of the peach

flavored black tea?"

"Sure do. I have a box I just bought with your name on it. I'll be out in a few," Phoebe said.

Chapter 3

In the throes of projects like this toll road segment, the work was a grind. For Mike, Bruno, and Ray, along with all the men that worked on it, it was sometimes hard to see the forest for the trees—the ultimate piece of road as it came to fruition. The road where there hadn't been one before they started. In Mike's position, he had a better 'vision' of things as they progressed, but only because of his thirty years' experience as a highway engineer. And after a project was done and maybe sometime later. Years even. And he saw what they'd done; maybe driving by or passing over in a company helicopter for a survey, he'd look and marvel.

"Did we really do that?" he'd say.

"It was a gift," he'd say too; that they could play a part in ventures so much bigger than themselves. He reminded his men of the same thing on those tough days when they had fights between them, equipment broke down, or corporate was riding their asses. But even that didn't always soothe. He was getting tired. The work was brutal. He'd said goodbye to the guys this afternoon and headed out. It was Friday, and they'd be back tomorrow. Saturday—a short day. Himself, Bruno, and about fifteen guys—a skeleton crew. They had a punch list of things to do before Monday. Some cleanup and prep work to make the day's work go smoother Monday. As he drove down the road, he looked around at the roadway, the greenery and remaining parts of forests that'd once been there.

"It's still nice. The birds have a place to rest and we'll have something to look at while we're driving. Other than the road," he thought.

"I'm done at sixty-two. Maybe even sixty," he said. Another six to eight years. It was in his blood, though. He shook his head and wondered if he'd ever be able to walk away from it. His father had his own medium-sized construction company, and he went until he was eighty. He was the owner, though, and could let others do some of his bidding if he needed rest. Mike shrugged and drove. His thoughts moving to dinner.

"Pizza tonight," he said. He headed to Stonehenge Finery. A new pizza place with 'high end' exotic pizzas. He just wanted a change and recently saw the Grand Opening sign.

"Probably'll be an arm and a leg for a pizza," he thought. He didn't care. Kiewit was stingy with their salaries, but as one of their top road engineers, he was still making over three hundred large annually, most of which went right into the bank. He could make more elsewhere, but the projects Kiewit got were more interesting. It was like working for Apple. It wasn't necessarily about the money, but what you could do there you couldn't do at other companies. He was treating his brother tonight, who was driving down to Virginia from Rhode Island. A social visit plus some hunting for a couple of weeks. It was open season in the state for three weeks with black powder. After dinner, they'd go back to Mike's house and his brother would stay with him for the duration. Mike's phone went off in his pocket. He looked at the phone. "It's Gavin," he said. He pressed the 'accept call' icon.

"Hey Gavin, how was your drive down?" Mike said.

"Good enough. Long, but no trouble. I got here early and dropped some of my stuff off near the outside of your house already. And I'm already here, Mike—at Stonehenge. This is a nice place, glad you suggested it. You ever been here?" he said.

"Nope. It just opened a couple of weeks ago. We both like pizza, so thought it'd be a good idea to try it out," he said.

"Tell me what you want. I'll order—"

"Gavin, it's on me, remember? Just hang—"

"I got it Mike. I'll be here for two weeks. You can take me to Ruth's Chris tomorrow. I'll get the pizza tonight. It's not as much as you thought it would, not that either of really care, right? I'm getting pepperoni, hot peppers and mushrooms on thin crust," Gavin said.

"You know what, that sound good. Same for me, but regular crust. Get a pitcher of Sam Adams dark ale too. I'm five minutes away," he said.

"Consider it done. Look forward to seeing you, big brother," he said.

Mike and his brother weren't twins, but sometimes people thought they were. Both big framed men. Gavin was younger, but not by much. Their mom and dad didn't play around. Born barely fifteen months apart, their mother was still nursing Mike when she got pregnant with Gavin. Gavin had an almost imperceptibly receding hairline, and he was maybe a mite bigger than Mike. Mike removed his hat when he walked into the restaurant and looked around. He saw Gavin waving at him. The table his brother was sitting at was one of those high numbers; similar to what they have in the bar area of Buffalo Wild Wings sports bars. He bounded over and Gavin stood. They gave each other a bear hug and looked at each other.

"Two, or is it three years now since I saw you last?" Mike said. Sitting down across from him.

"Three. But who's counting? Good to see you Mike. You look great. Older but great," Gavin said.

"Thanks for the compliment," he said. They laughed. It was true though—neither of them were getting any younger.

"How's Patricia?" Mike said.

"Doing well. She's the one that urged me to come down. She knows I love you almost as much as I love hunting," he said. Peering at his brother over the frame of his glasses.

"There're no mats here, but I should take you down for that, you know?" Mike said.

"It's not worth it. You know I'd kick your ass," Gavin said. They were both wrestlers in high school. They'd broken a good few pieces of furniture in their home when they were younger. Mike shook his head. "You probably would, wouldn't you? You look great too Gavin, and I'm glad Patricia sent you down."

"Yeah. She's something else. Great wife and still hasn't thrown me out. How about a toast," he said. Gavin poured each of them a cold ale and held up his glass. They clinked glasses and took a drink of the icy cold foam topped dark ale.

"Ahh, good stuff," Mike said. Their waitress brought their pizzas and set them down on their table.

"Anything else, guys?" she said. They looked at each other and shook their heads.

"We're all set. Thanks much," Mike said. They dug in and ate. The pizzas looked fantastic. They cooked the crusts well done. After a bit Gavin looked at Mike, "have you met anyone?"

"Gavin, I'm married to Kiewit. And highway construction. If I met anyone, she'd already've divorced me," he said. It wasn't totally untrue. He'd had a girlfriend or two over the last few years. They all dumped him. Not that they didn't like him. To know Mike was to love him. But he never had any time. Lots of cancelled dinner and lunch engagements. The 'short' Saturdays often turned into another long day. He couldn't spend the time the girls needed. He wanted the same as they did, but it seemed impossible. Gavin nodded but felt bad for his brother. He knew he'd be a great catch for a woman that could endure his schedule. And work with him, take him when he was available.

"Patricia couldn't do it," he thought. But he knew there were women that would—for the right man.

"Mike, why don't you come out with me on Sunday? We can make it a short day so you can get some rest before Monday. I've already considered the areas that most hunters don't like. That's where the deer'll be. There's a spot not even ninety minutes from your house. Let's go early and I'll have you back by four. Probably earlier," he said. He knew his brother loved hunting as much as he did. It was tough for him to get out, though. Mike was chewing a mouthful of pizza, which he rinsed down with a swallow of ale. He remembered he didn't go three years ago when his brother came and was sorry he didn't. He enjoyed sleeping in on Sunday. Gavin saw him thinking.

"Mike, you're a natural. Not just a great shot, too. You know how to 'hunt.' And we're not getting any younger. Patrica told me to come down a couple of days early so we could go out. I planned it all to make it easy for you," he said. He stopped and waited, looking across the table at his brother.

"I can sleep when I retire. I'm going with you," he said. Gavin nodded energetically, a big smile on his face.

"Yes. Mike, that's great. It means the world to me we're going together. I brought down both my black powder rifles. I don't mind sharing one, but this way neither of us needs to be a bystander," he said. Gavin was genuinely pumped. Mike was glad he was going too. Life was too short, and he didn't want to blow it again and not go this time. He intended on making sure tomorrow, Saturday, at the site was kept to a 'short day,' even if it killed him to do it.

"What time are we leaving?" Mike asked. He meant Sunday morning.

"You're not gonna like it—we drive out of your driveway at four am. I'm trying to be helpful to you. I'd normally be out—"

"Bro, we need to get out at three. I know that's when we need to leave. Let's do it right. I don't need to be babied. Much as I appreciate it, but we both know if there's any hope of getting some antlers—anything we'd be proud to hang up —we gotta get out early," he said. Gavin smiled.

"Plus, I won't be able to sleep anyway after taking you to Ruth's Chris tomorrow night," he said.

"Mike, you want to show me the roadway?" he said. He meant the section of road he was working on right now.

"How about tomorrow? We'll go up together. It'll make it easier for me to break away if you're with me," Mike said.

"Sure. Good plan. Are we done here or you want a throw another one down?" Gavin said.

"No, let's get out of here. It was great pizza, but it's time to go home now. I got some cans of Coors in the fridge," he said.

"I'm telling you, someone's been in the system. I can see the 'shadow' of someone being in here. It's a kind of electronic trail, but I can't 'see' what they were looking at. Like someone who half knows what they're doing. Not that it'd be easy to ghost the system—be 'invisible,' that is. It's one of the best in law enforcement." It was Vince Romano of the Henrico County Police Department. He ran and operated their information security database system. The system was designed primarily to assist in criminal investigations. But it could also find any person's 'unlisted' phone numbers, their physical location or whereabouts of people, based on license plate tracking, facial recognition, credit card usage and other data points people normally wouldn't think could be used to find them. Vince was clicking the keyboard and typing different obscure commands.

"Nothing's coming up," he said.

"What made you go looking?" Shelby said. She was a department admin assigned to the building's front desk. A medium height wafer thin redhead, with flaming red hair and a good eye for details. Vince called her 'Red.' Since she liked him, he let her get a way with it.

"I'm not sure, Red. An ever so brief pause at a screen when I first log in, maybe a refresh flicker not normally there or that seemed different. This is like my firstborn child—this system. I know it and how it behaves. And I have a good nose," he said. Vince Romano was a former New Jersey longshoreman. Work that often seemed to put you right in the thick of crime, graft, underhanded dealings and, worst of all, crime bosses.

"If you're anywhere near those guys when they bust anyone, you'll be pulled in too, Vince. Even if you're 'cleared,' you'll have a record. It'll louse up your entire future. Unless you want to be a longshoreman fixture or a Teamsters underboss. Anything else, you're probably done," his father said. He got his 'nose' from Dad, who was sure there was something going on at the docks. Little whiffs and snippets of things he'd read and heard. He warned Vince. Told him he could just come home, take a break and think about what he wanted to do. Fortunately, he listened to his father and gave a one week notice. "Family member with a serious health problem, etc." His brother had a bad flu. It's entirely possible it could've gotten worse.

"You sure you want to leave, kid? Hard to get back in once you walk," his manager told him. He was part of the operation and they needed kids like Vince, who did their bidding but didn't know what was actually going on.

"I really appreciate it, Enzo. My father told me the same thing, but I have to take care of family. Maybe down the road sometime I'll check in, see what you've got, etc, etc. Old Dad was right, though in the end. There'd be no more 'checking in.' At least not with his manager or anyone else near his level. All of them ended up on long term 'leave' at Rikers Island or San Quentin.

"Vince, you got a good nose, too. Like me. Your Mom and me, we saved up some money. Why don't you enroll at Long Island Technical? Study something there, maybe get a decent job somewhere," Dad said. Vince took him up on it. Studied computer and internet security. He had a gift. He ate up the tech school and became almost otherworldly proficient at computer security. Internet protocols, routers, sleuthing, sniffing and tracking. He looked like a Teamsters enforcer but was a modern day Sherlock Holmes on a computer.

"Hey Red, don't let anyone know I found anything. You know, Mum's the word ok?"

"What's it worth to you?" she said. She was leaning over his shoulder, looking at the screen. Vince shook his head, but was smiling.

"How about lunch and a coffee tomorrow?" he said.

"Deal. My lips are sealed," she said.

"Hey, one more thing. Let me know if you see anyone in particular taking an interest in the system," he said. She winked and nodded at him and went to her desk.

"I'll find out who you are and what you're doing. Or my name's not Vince Romano," he said under his breath. He clicked off the monitor and headed over to the morning department meeting.

Chapter 4

Phoebe left early to run some errands before she went to work for the day. Her sister was still at the house and she wanted to pick up a few things for her so she wouldn't have to leave and could relax for the day. In other words, keep a low profile. She'd run the items back, then leave for work. She knew she couldn't stop her sister from running out and didn't care if she did. But with that bastard out there, wherever he is, she thought she could make it so she could chill at the house for the day if she wanted to.

"Almost done," Phoebe thought. She stopped at Kroger and was now leaving CVS, which was her last stop and heading to her car.

"Home, then to work," she said. She set the bag down in the passenger seat as she was getting in the car.

"Having a good day, Phoebe? Looks like you're doing some early morning shopping." It was a man's voice. Someone standing closer than they should be. Phoebe's pulse began racing before she even saw who it was. Turning to see Cam, her sister's ex-husband, standing right there.

"Don't get up on my account. I just happened to be here and thought I'd come over and say hi," he said. Visibly shaken, she looked at Rick Cameron's smiling face, who

24

stood so close she couldn't close her car door.

"What the hell do you want, you creep?" she said. The sugar-coated version of what she wanted to say.

"Now that's not very friendly, is it?" he said.

"Look asshole, leave me and my sister alone. Do you understand?"

"I hear what you're saying, but you shouldn't be so rude, you know? I'm just trying to be cordial," he said. Then he leaned closer to her and stood in a way that prevented her from closing the door or getting out of the car.

"Tell your sister I just wanted to say 'hello.' And I miss her. I hope she has a pleasant visit up here while she's staying at your place. The reason I'm telling you personally is I can't seem to reach her on her phone," he said.

"I'm not telling her shit, asshole. Now move so I can go," she said. Rick Cameron stood where he was and braced himself, holding the door. He looked at his ex sister-in-law. She was scared and looked down. She knew her sister's ex was a very dangerous man. In a slow and controlled manner, he moved away from the door, keeping his hand on the top edge while he did.

"Have a nice day, Phoebe. I'll see you around." He let go of the door and walked away. Phoebe could tell even from the side view he was smirking. Phoebe was shaking so badly she had to just sit. She tried to see what car he was driving, but he walked around to the other side of the CVS. After sitting a couple of minutes, she drove away. Phoebe didn't want to stay where she was in case he was still there on the other side. She pulled into a strip mall on the way to her house and parked near some other cars. She unbuckled her seatbelt, sat there and breathed. Her pulse was pounding hard, and she was shaking. She looked at her phone to check the time.

"I'll be late for work," she said. She knew if she told her sister what happened, she'd leave and go home to Atlanta.

"If the asshole's going to harass her, or us, I want to be with her when he does," she said. Phoebe knew it had to a living hell married to this guy. And she doubted he was going away anytime soon. Still shaking, she started the car and drove home.

"Took you a little while, Phoebe. You didn't really have to do this for me, you know," she said.

"I wanted to. And it's for me too. Some stuff we can have later when I get home from work. I'm running late though now and'll have to scoot. You gonna be ok?" Phoebe said.

"Yeah. I think I'll be fine. How about you, Phoebe? You seem agitated." Phoebe shook her head. Her sister didn't miss much either.

"I'm ok. I ran a red light by mistake and thought I'd seen a cruiser. Shook me up a minute, but I'll be fine," she said. Hating to tell her sister something that wasn't so. But she didn't want her to leave her.

"All right. I'm off to work. I'll be home early. Maybe we'll go get something to eat out tonight," she said.

"I'd love to go out later. I'll put all these things away and see you when you get here. And hey, thanks Phoebe," she said. Phoebe stood and looked at her. It killed her how a woman as dignified and good-hearted as her sister could ever have married a man she considered a criminal thug.

"Love you Sis. See you later," she said. Phoebe thought about women she'd known, some she'd read about and others from news stories. How men like Cam terrorize ex wives or girlfriends, even hurting them physically or murdering them. It was always the same MO. Some smart psycho who made sure they had the drop on a woman, to guarantee they couldn't defend themselves. And for some twisted or perverted reason, don't even see themselves for what they are. Human scum, that in other societies, would probably be summarily shot by the girl's father. She shook her head, wondering how it could be that people like him could be out walking the streets at all. She also knew that since Cameron knew she was visiting her, he also knew where her house was. The whole thing infuriated her.

"How could he find out all these things? Addresses and phone numbers. And where I was this morning? He probably followed me and I didn't notice," she thought. She thought about how convenient it would be if she knew a real life Michael Corleone who could 'help her out. With a favor.'

"Only in the movies," she said.

Officer Royland Whitman was a mid-level police officer on the force. He stood in his civilian clothes outside a warehouse district downtown, smoking a cigarette. A Marlboro Red. Smoking wasn't permitted in uniform. It used to be allowed on breaks, but it'd been years since that was true. And even to get hired now, you had to be a nonsmoker. You had to admit, under oath, you weren't a smoker, plus they tested your blood and urine before they officially hired you. They knew some officers who'd gotten in under the old system smoked. Grandfathered in, but you still had to abide by the 'never any smoking in uniform' requirement. Roy wasn't a smoker when he first joined the force. He smoked when he was a teen in high school and also when he worked at the sheet metal plant afterwards. By the time he was in college for his associate's degree in criminal justice, he'd long since quit. After that he applied to become a police officer. And for Roy, along with most people that'd smoked once then quit, it took a major event—something extremely stressful—to 'trip' the urge to start smoking again. And many former smokers developed a visceral hatred of smoking and probably could never start up again under any condition. Roy's switch tripped, though. He started smoking again after the 'incident.' The shooting itself wasn't the problem particularly. It was the short-term aftermath. Then it became the long-term aftermath.

"Brain cancer would be better than this," he said. He was far away from the usual patrol and working areas of Henrico County. Not that a stray officer or civilian who knew him couldn't've spotted him. But it wasn't likely where he was right now. Standing there smoking, he waited for a phone call. There was a window of time he'd make himself available. No call came. It didn't always. Roy flung the spent cigarette butt onto the ground and powered off the phone as he walked away.

"It's killing me," he thought. It was almost ten years ago now. A young officer, he'd received a call from dispatch; a domestic fight or abuse situation a neighbor called in. It was by the airport, and in that neighborhood, they always sent two patrol cars. Roy arrived first and the second car, not even a minute later. Roy started to the house following proper protocol on approach. The backup vehicle officer was standing by his car. The flashers of both cars were on silently as Roy made his way to the house. It was a single family dwelling and he could hear the machinations of a screaming match between a man and woman inside. Roy enjoyed being a police officer, but preferred more routine matters rather than potential violent encounters. He was good with the kids. The young men who were wayward—or headed that way. This situation could be a shouting match or it could be a dangerous physical slugfest. The danger is people involved in a domestic often preferred to work out their own matters. When a neighbor or outsider calls the police, it can have the unfortunate effect of increasing tensions. This is the part that could trip someone over the edge. He stood by the door and heard some slamming inside and a woman's voice talking. "I'm leaving right now. I'll come back when you sober up," she screamed. A back door banged when she went out.

He knocked on the door.

"Police. Open up please," he said. Roy was nervous and couldn't help keeping his hand near his gun. He looked behind him and the officer outside nodded. A 'keep going' gesture, though he'd moved a little closer towards the house. The way it all played out was a man opened the door and looked out. Bleary and obviously had been drinking.

"Yeah, what is it?" he said.

"Someone called and said there was a disturbance here," he said. Roy noticed that the man had one of his hands behind him.

"Sir, I need you to put both hands where I can see them, please," he said. The man in the house was Roderigo Gaston, who, though a drunk and usually good for a big verbal fight with his wife, wasn't really prone to physical violence. Of course, no police officer knows what they're dealing with during an altercation, traffic stop, or even a 'homeless' vagrant. Roderigo had an empty Coke bottle—a glass one, and he'd been making gestures with it. Smacking it in his hand when he was arguing with his wife. It was stupid for sure, he knew. He hated himself for even implying he'd strike his wife with it. Anyway, what happened next was fuzzy. Roderigo Gaston intended to drop the bottle on the floor. He hesitated too long. Drunk as he was, and he made a hurried movement to hold the door for a moment so he could fling the bottle behind him. Instead, he opened the door inadvertently and in the process swung his other arm around because he'd lost his balance. Roy already had his hand near his gun, pretty much on it. To him, he thought he was about to be physically assaulted and gun at the ready. The Coke bottle 'looked' like a weapon and Roy fired. A single shot in Roderigo's upper torso. Close to his thorax. The single bullet hit his spine and killed him close to instantly. Roy saw and heard the Coke bottle clatter to the floor as Roderigo Gaston fell backwards. Dead moments after he struck the floor.

Roy was horrified at what happened and for a moment stood there. Swinging any sort of weapon, club, bottle piece of pipe. Almost anything really could still be grounds for an 'acceptable,' or justifiable police shooting. One that wouldn't necessarily destroy a career in law enforcement. Assessing a tense situation is easier from an armchair than in the thick of it. He holstered his gun, standing back. His ears were ringing from the shot and at first he didn't even realize there were steps coming from behind him. The backup officer walked past him and made a gesture for him to stand still and wait. Backup walked into the house and looked around, thinking. On the kitchen counter was a knife. A bigger type used for cutting up vegetables. He picked it up with a hand towel laying nearby and placed it into the deceased man's hand and pressed his fingers around it using the towel then let it go. He kicked the knife a few inches away, set the towel on the counter. Looked around and came over to Roy.

"I saw the whole thing. He took a swing at you with a knife and you shot him. Open and shut. Relax Whitman," he said. He patted him on the shoulder.

"Want me to call it in or you want to?" he added. Roy licked his lips and tried to stop himself from sweating. He turned and looked at Backup.

"You do it," he said.

"Good idea. Go sit in your car. I'll take it from here," Backup said.

The official report was pretty much the way Backup said it would be. There was an investigation. Body cameras weren't being used then. It looked about right. There were a couple of minor discrepancies that the crime scene photographer noted. He wasn't an investigator but asked about the empty Coke bottle nearby on the floor; ultimately brushed off as household litter. Something that hadn't gotten picked up. There was also the fact that the prints on the knife handle didn't quite look right for a grip a person would use if they were swinging it or attacking someone. In the end, though, it was 'close enough.' It was a fringe neighborhood anyway, with a fair amount of rabble known to be present. The case was wrapped up, the closing investigation was a peremptory affair. Mainly just to close out the shooting, the conclusion basically already made. There were other more pressing cases in the community and the captain wanted everything wrapped up asap. The wife's ramblings about how "my husband would never hurt anyone, and he was all bark, no bite etc etc," were dismissed as 'trailer park trash talk.' Roy's career as a police officer was intact. The shooting was considered justifiable, and the books were closed.

There was only one matter Roy Whitman didn't consider in the harrowing days following the initial shooting until the books were finally closed on the investigation. And they took him off of paid administrative leave, returning to full capacity duty on the force. Backup that afternoon was Officer Richard Cameron. 'Cam,' as he was commonly called.

Chapter 5

Rick Cameron was a patient man. But even at the time of his department police officer partner shooting, the fringes were fraying on his career with the County Police. Only a few people saw it. Those few recognizing that Officer Richard Cameron had some problems. There were some arrests where the use of excessive force seemed unreasonable. He'd hurt a couple of suspects a lot more than it appeared at first, in the process of arrest and transport. A concussion on one male taken in wasn't obvious. In jail, the man stated repeatedly he had a terrible headache and the officer that arrested him hurt him. He'd told them he didn't resist arrest and was trying to be cooperative. Officer Cameron struck his head on the back of the plexiglass divider in the car. But he's done it in such a way there was no obvious evidence. The arrestee had done nothing particularly to tweak Officer Cameron but did have a slight gimp and wasn't moving as fast as Cameron had wanted. So he gave him a 'hand' and 'helped him' into the squad car. What wasn't known was the argument; or a better way to put it was the fight he had with his wife that morning. One of the many he'd had with her, which were escalating in intensity lately.

His wife's father was always wary of him and advised her, even when she'd first met him, to move on while she could.

"I have a bad feeling about him, Honey. It's easy to get out now. You know I'm not one to make this decision for you—who to marry or date. He 'looks' respectable. Like a strong and purposeful man. But there's something I sense that isn't right. Some sort of loose screw. I don't know," he said. She never listened. It's the way love is. Like other lessons in life, only after you do what's inadvisable do you learn.

Every officer has a bad day now and again. Like any other person. And maybe he or she is a bit too aggressive or rough once in a while. Usually nothing more than a hard shove into the car. Maybe grab a suspect's arm too fast. Something like that. Not actual brutality, though.

Rick Cameron continued to decline. Frustrated at what he thought was his wife's being overly 'concerned' about him. Then it became maddening. And he'd retrieved over one voice message from her father expressing his concern over 'her situation.' Not leaving any details, but he knew it was about him. When he confronted her about it, she'd try to calm him down, but he had a way of working himself up into a rage. The first steps were smashing things, like their stereo. Then punching a hole in the wall. Then advanced to cornering his wife, where she could tell he was within a hair's breadth of striking her. Anything she did seemed to make him worse. Then he finally started. The first time, punching her in the stomach. It was a 'small' punch, but properly placed to inflict as much pain and discomfort as possible. He towered over her as she lay holding her stomach on the floor. He didn't want to hurt her, but seemed incapable of stopping himself. In time, the events escalated. Rick Cameron didn't trust himself and didn't trust his wife.

The situation grew worse and at the advice of her sister Phoebe; she gathered medical reports and photographs of her injuries. Textbook incidents of severe spousal abuse. Phoebe ran interference with one of the best attorneys in the state and he said two documented incidents were enough to execute an incontestable divorce and put him away forever. She had three recorded and photographed events; the last involved three broken ribs that were so damaged, they were pulling away from the internal cartilage at the junction of her rib cage. They were always injuries that weren't visible walking around with clothes on.

It wasn't pretty; the divorce. Phoebe and her father were there. Rick Cameron couldn't have been more distinguished at the hearing in the attorney's executive meeting room. The picture of decency. His father-in-law didn't buy it and neither did anyone else there other than possibly his own attorney who was with him. He'd seen the evidence himself, wincing when he did. He was damage control. That was the best he'd be able to do.

"They're doing you a favor, Mr. Cameron. I hope you understand," he'd said.

"I got the whole world up my ass. I don't need you up there either," he said. A real prize. His attorney would be glad when it was all over. There were also two off-duty policemen hired to act as guards outside the room. Phoebe encouraged her sister to throw the book at him and bring the case to court.

"Destroy his career and put him away," she said. Sis shook her head.

"It would be worse to do that. A lot worse. He'd eventually get out; even if they sent him to prison. Then he'd be on a full rampage. This is already going to be bad enough. I'm not trying to hurt him. I just don't want him to hurt me. Hopefully, he'll appreciate it," she'd said. He didn't. He'd also threatened to take the case to court to his attorney, who wisely advised it would then be on public record. And basically a guarantee of being terminated by the police force, along with never being able to get work in any official capacity as a law enforcement officer. For once Rick Cameron understood. The papers were all signed, the divorce completed, and they wrapped it up. Phoebe looked across the table at him, an angry expression in her eyes. His wife remained calm and dignified. She had no malice in her face nor pity. The same could not be said for her and Phoebe's father, who flatly glared across at Cameron. He knew a dangerous man when he saw one and bad as he thought Richard Cameron was as a man, he never thought he'd inflict physical harm on his daughter. He was the only person in the room Rick Cameron was afraid of. In a rare instance for Rick Cameron, he averted his eyes from his wife's father.

"Ok, we're done here today. A distasteful matter, but now we move on. Richard Cameron, your attorney and assistant, may leave first, per the terms of protocol disclosed before we started," It was the senior partner of the firm who'd come in to dismiss the meeting as an 'uninterested' party to the proceedings. The two double wide doors were opened and the two off-duty police officers, hired from a different county in the state, stood by. They didn't know who anyone was and their sole purpose was to act as enforcement if there were any difficulties. They were armed and in nearly complete capacity as officers, sanctioned by their department. As Rick Cameron, his attorney and assistant left, one of the off-duty officers made the slightest movement of his head towards them as they walked down the hallway out of the suite. The other nodded ever so mildly. With an 'I know. He's the reason we're here,' expression on his face.

"You can dress `em up but they're still the same underneath," the first one thought to himself. Rick Cameron was required to be a driven as a passenger by his attorney to his wife's attorney's office. Once the office assistant notified them they'd driven off, the attorney handling the case for Phoebe, her sister, and father sat down with them.

"I appreciate your trust in using our firm for handling this egregious and disheartening matter. The marriage is dissolved and you, madam, are 'free' now," he said. Pausing with his hands clasped in front of him. He looked at the girl's father, then the two women, knowing it was the one sister, Phoebe Rinnder, and her father, that started the case.

"I wish I could say it's over. And, in a sense, it is. You're officially divorced. However, I also know men like this sometimes persist. That's the one problem I can't help you with. I wish I could and am sorry for everything that's happened to you all. You've said you plan on keeping us on retainer, and we're grateful. But I would recommend considering an identity change and maybe even move out of the state to you, Mrs. Cameron. It's troublesome, I know. Other than that, we're here to assist. We have a discreet organization that is an affiliate of ours who can assist you with that course of action if you choose to consider it. Call us here and Rose, my administrative assistant, will provide everything you need. And of course, I'll make myself available as well," he said. Their father reminded him of his own sixty-eight year old dad. He hated to think what his own father would do to a man that did what this man had done to his sister. He stood. Then their father, Mr. Rinnder, followed suit, extending his hand across the table to the attorney, not saying anything, and looked him squarely in the eyes. He nodded his thanks and didn't speak. Afraid that, between his anger and sadness, he'd break down right there. He looked at his daughters and they followed him out of the office and left.

Rick Cameron's wife was forty-five, Phoebe forty-three, and their father sixty-six the day they walked out of the attorney's office. At Phoebe's insistence, her sister changed her name and moved to a suburb outside of Atlanta. It was far away and a beautiful developing area. Plus, Phoebe had a soft spot for Atlanta and thought she could visit her sister there. The years went by and it seemed like their troubles were all past them. An excellent plan.

The Henrico County Police learned Rick Cameron had gotten divorced. It happened. He wasn't the only police officer that'd ever gotten one. Officer Rick Cameron decided he'd 'turn over a new leaf.' And initially he tried. But bitterness about the divorce and the exposure and shame his wife'd put him through ate at him. He lost sight of how easy his wife and her attorney were on him. Then there was another incident while he was on duty. An arrest of a drunk that resulted in some injuries. Someone in Internal Affairs took notice and pulled out his files. It might not have even gotten this far if Rick Cameron had simply made a personal apology to the person and his mother. That was the mother's request.

"I did nothing. He resisted arrest, and I used 'reasonable force' to detain him etc," was how he'd presented it. The problem was the mother's ex, himself a former police officer, talked to his son and ex-wife about it when she'd complained to him that the officer or department wouldn't apologize. Something didn't seem right to him because he knew his son, even when he'd been drinking, was a decent good-natured person. He filed a formal query with Henrico County Police. One thing led to the other and Sharon Wilder, the IAD investigator from hell, put together a case file. She gave her preliminary findings to Captain Mattias, who passed on the fact there would be an investigation to Cameron's Sergeant and that Cameron would need to be questioned as well as other members of the department who worked with him, etc.

"Who's the investigator?" Sergeant Jamison said.
"Open up the file," the captain said. Jamison looked at the top page.

"Shit. You're kidding me," he said. He closed the file, then opened it again. Jamison was in the Captain's office and looked behind him, to make sure the door was closed.

"We may as well just shoot the guy; it'd be less painful," he said. Captain Mattias smiled. He knew what he meant. If there was anything there. Anything. Sharon Wilder would find it. In fact, it was safe to say if she was onto you, you'd almost be better shooting yourself to save all the trouble.

"All right, I'll let him know. I'll cooperate, of course. We all will, right? Or we'll be next," Jamison said.

"Right," Mattias said. Jamison folded up the file and stood, getting ready to leave.

"Jamison, there's something about this guy that's troubled me. An event I brushed aside as an idle arrest complaint a couple of years ago. We should've looked into it ourselves when it happened. What I wanted to say, though, is Cameron is trouble. I can see it myself in this file. It's not worth your neck or mine to cover or protect this guy. Do you understand?" he said.

"Loud and clear, Captain," he said. Mattias gave an abrupt wave and Jamison left the office.

Jamison asked his secretary in to his office and explained to her any resistance by those being questioned in this matter would be subject to administrative action and possible unpaid leave.

"Make sure everyone understands," he said. Jamison handed her the folder and the names of officers that were to be called in for questioning that she was to arrange. She nodded and looked at the paper, then looked at Jamison.

"Wilder?" she said.

"Right," he said. There was no one that wasn't new in the department that didn't 'know' who Sharon Wilder was and what it meant if she was onto you.

"Sergeant, maybe this doesn't matter, but I found out about

it from a public source. Officer Cameron's wife divorced him over a year ago for severely beating her on multiple occasions. I'm not willing to work to protect him. I'll resign before I help cover for him in—"

"Katie, I got it. And I wouldn't want you to. I've had it too 'helping' officers who deserve to get thrown out. I'd be right behind you. And if that's not enough, Mattias said he wants 'full cooperation' from everyone. Ok?" he said.

"Yeah. Good, thanks," she said. Katie knew IAD would sometimes look for a scapegoat. Wilder was brutal, but honest—she came after you if you deserved it. But definitely brutal. Secretly, Katie never liked Rick Cameron and hoped he'd be tossed or even arrested himself.

Chapter 6

Rick Cameron had extraordinary tenacity. Even knowing the players, the stakes and especially Sharon Wilder, he still managed to put the system through the ringer. In that, he didn't make it easy for them. Using every provision for technical consideration of guilt to delay, prolong, and frustrate the process. He was a strong opponent against Sharon Wilder, except for one thing; he didn't have truth on his side. It didn't help either, that he'd angered several people on the force, who'd eventually moved into more important positions. In the end, though, he was found guilty of police brutality and dismissed from the police force. Rather than be arrested and tried, he'd gotten one last 'favor,' from the former police captain who'd retired when Rick Cameron was just new with Henrico County. Using what little influence he had left as a former captain, he requested a non-arrest dismissal of Cameron. Older now and not interested as much in the current state of affairs, the department reluctantly agreed to the prior captain's last request. A real feat and against the wishes of Sergeant Jamison and Sharon Wilder, who made it known in the record it was a mistake in her opinion and would be a probable cause of problems for the county in the future. Which would later prove to be true.

Once again, though, Rick Cameron didn't internalize or acknowledge the 'gift' he'd received by not being formally charged; and only being released without charges being formally brought to bear. There'd be no public record of the termination; just like his divorce. Rather than consider he'd be able to still make a go of himself, he instead seethed with anger.

"It's all her fault. And her meddling sister," is what he thought. Fueled by hatred and anger, he never seemed able to reconcile anything as being his own problem. For the time being, he got work as a contract security guard. The work suited him. They mainly left him alone, and there wasn't usually any real trouble. If there was, he was intimidating enough to solve most any difficulties, such as vagrants, thefts, or simply breaking and entering. But Rick Cameron missed the power of the State behind him. That's what he loved about being an actual police officer, the 'official' state authority.

The next few years seemed to go by uneventfully. Rick Cameron was one of the private guard company's meanest 'junkyard dogs,' as they called them. Men that, for whatever reason, were not unnerved at all to work on the worst or most dangerous district assignments. The pay was pretty good too. After a time he'd almost gotten it close to the $60k a year, he was making as a Henrico County police officer. And as he settled down into his routine, he decided he'd try to look up his wife and see if he could get in touch with her to say 'hello.' The divorce agreement prohibited it, but since they settled it out of a courtroom, he knew there were no actual 'teeth' in the edict. It was a complete dead end. He couldn't find her name, address or phone number. Nothing.

"That bitch Phoebe," he said. He knew she and her father were surely behind it.

"Maybe she's with her old man now," he thought. Then realized it wouldn't be like her to do that; "Go live with Dad again." He fumed over the matter and tried to convince himself to just drop it and leave it alone.

"I've got a job now. Decent pay. Almost a clean slate," he thought. He couldn't let it go. One evening after a late night shift, he was at his apartment going through some of his things. Looking for ideas. In a box of his belonging's he pulled out a file he didn't realize he still had. It was a police folder, a report he'd somehow had in his personal car that he failed to file when he was still on the force. Rick Cameron opened it and started flipping through the pages. A smile formed on his face as he read the details, and former officer Cameron started nodding.

"Perfect. This is just perfect. It's exactly what I need," he said. He wrote some notes down on a separate piece of paper and looked at his phone to check his schedule.

"My next shift is midnight tomorrow. I've got plenty of time to get this started before then," he thought. He set aside his notes and tucked the file away; thinking it was a gift that he still had it.

Rick Cameron sat in his car outside Roy Whitman's home. He was down the block, about ten cars away. Whitman was an ok cop but wouldn't notice he was there. Cameron didn't know what Whitman's schedule was; but he'd find out. The old-fashioned way, with a crude stakeout. It didn't matter if it took him a couple of days. He'd never forgotten about Roy Whitman. But he never really knew the guy, and they ushered him out of the department so fast, there was no way he could go around and collect personal phone numbers on his way out the door. Fortunately, Whitman's address was on public record and courtesy of Google, Cameron was sitting outside the house right now. He could've called the number he'd found but thought it could be his wife's or maybe the house number. If he didn't answer, Cameron could just end up being reported and possibly picked up for questioning.

"Nothing beats a personal meeting anyway," he said. Cameron checked the time.

"Close to four. I'll give it three more hours, then try a different time range tomorrow," he thought. He half rested and lay his head back, thinking he'd just leave, anyway. That's when he saw Whitman. He was coming down the road in a county cruiser. Cameron waited until Whitman parked and went into his house.

"Must be on a break. Odd time to be off," he said. But he was here now, and that's all that mattered. Cameron walked towards the house after waiting five minutes and knocked on the door. He heard walking inside and the door opened. Whitman was in uniform and looked at him.

"Cam. What are you doing here?" he said.

"What's the matter Roy? Aren't you happy to see me?" he said. Whitman looked behind him into the house. Then turned back to Cameron.

"What is it Rick? Why are you here?" he said.

"I want to talk with you. It'll only take a couple of minutes," he said. It wasn't a request.

"Wait here a minute. I'll come outside," he said.

"Sure. But Roy, make sure you come back out. I'll wait, ok?" he said.

"Yeah, no problem. I'll be right back, ok?" he said. Whitman was home for a 'hello' visit to his wife to have a coffee together. Still on duty until around seven. He came right back out after telling his wife he'd be a few minutes. He hoped he'd never see Rick Cameron again. Whitman's heart sank when he opened the door and saw him. He remembered how relieved he was when he was tossed from the force, too. He braced himself when he walked back out.

"Ok Cam, all set. What brings you by?" It was a stupid question. He knew Cameron wanted something and was sorry he said it. Cameron was quiet for a moment until they were further down the road.

"Whitman, I'll make this easy for you. We don't need to waste a lot of time here and I won't revisit your shooting from way back when. I'll just proceed ok?" he said.

"Of course," Whitman said. He was sick now, thinking how much he wished he'd done things differently then. Even without Rick Cameron showing, he already lived in disgust with himself. Henrico might've dismissed him, but it wouldn't've been a police coverup. His heart raced, waiting to hear what Cameron wanted.

"Back when, I remember hearing you had a knack for IT stuff. I haven't been able to get in touch with my ex-wife and wanted to at least be able to wish her a merry Christmas and a happy birthday. Just to let her know I care and tell her if she needs anything to let me know. She might be remarried for all I know and I misplaced her old number. I need you to find her for me and just get me her phone numbers. Any cell or home number plus her address and maybe her new married name. Ok?" Whitman was quiet, his heart was pounding. They were walking along, having already passed Rick's car.

"Rick look, I don't know, man. That's—"

"It's not a request, Whitman. I'll give you a week to get it for me. And I'll make it easy for you; give me your cell and I'll call you. You tell me when's a good time," he said. The threat was implicit and Whitman knew he had no actual choice but to do what he wanted. He wondered if anything Cameron said would be accepted as the truth, anyway. But he knew they tossed Cameron for brutality and a record of questionable situations while he was an officer. Worse, it was Wilder in IAD who ran the investigation. If his name came up in connection with Cameron, he knew he'd be next.

"Cam, it's not easy, but give me a few days. Call me Saturday at around six. Five days from now. Here's my number," he said. He showed Cameron his cell number, who dialed right then, so they each had a record of their phone numbers.

"Ok good. We're finished here. I'll call you when you said. And by the way, Whitman, I may need a few other things down the road. This is enough for now though," he said. Whitman nodded and walked back to his house. Trapped.

Rick Cameron could do a lot with the information he wanted from Whitman. Not everything he wished he could; no longer active duty, he couldn't use the patrol car scanners or access location records dynamically to find people at any given moment.

"It'll be enough for now though," he said. He waited until he saw Whitman go into his house, then walked to his car and drove in the opposite direction out of the neighborhood.

"Time for dinner, then work in several hours. A good day already," he thought.

Whitman was grateful Cameron didn't know that he'd once trained for a short while on how to use the police and FBI security system. He had an inclination for IT and was considering cross training into that specialty. Unknown to him, though, there were some individuals who had doubts about his character and ethics based on their personal interactions with him. Nothing definite but some wariness. They didn't come right out and say it, but used some other rationale. "We have more than enough staff working this area now." Or something similar and he was told he wouldn't be able to cross over at this time, etc. He moved on and proceeded as a regular officer

"What's the matter, Honey?' his wife said when he'd gone back in the house. She could tell right away he was dispirited.

"It was an old friend. A former officer from the force. He stopped by to say hello," he said.

"Ok. Well, I made us some coffee," she said. She thought maybe there was more to it than what he said. She wondered why he didn't just call her husband, but knew she wouldn't be able to pry anything else out of him. He'd already started smoking occasionally again a couple of years ago, so thought there was something bothering him already.

Chapter 7

Vince Romano peered at his computer screen, typing some commands and also referring to a notepad near him with some passwords and internet DNS addresses written on it. The passwords were useless by themselves unless you knew the other items he already had memorized.

"Whatcha lookin' at?" Vince smiled and turned. He already knew who it was. Shelby Gallagher was leaning awfully close to him as she looked at the screen. She didn't understand what it was and though she cared, mainly she wanted to get near Vince.

"Hey Good Lookin', I got him. Or at least he's finished now. Whoever it is that's been in here is blocked. I can't tell who it was, but his electronic access is blocked. He or she won't be able to get in anymore," he said.

"I got something for you," she said.

"What is it?" he said. She pulled up a roller chair and sat down so she could look at him. She looked around the office, then turned to Vince.

"I smelled cigarette smoke odor near the master terminal for the system in the secure storage room. I had to go in there and get some files and smelled residual smoke. When I walked around to see where it was, it was the strongest near the terminal. I don't know who it was, but I know this; one of the last people out of the room this morning was Officer Roy Whitman. He's a smoker. Hired under the old system. He can smoke off duty if he's not in uniform. He's not supposed to smoke in uniform, but they all do," she said. Vince stared at Gallagher and shook his head a little.

"Red, that's good. Unbelievable. The guy must know something about 'erasing' his tracks or I would've seen his login." Gallagher bounced a little in her chair, smiling. Thrilled, she could help Vince. She had a nose for details already, but it was good to have some sort of idea what they were looking for.

"Gallagher, he'll never get back in now if it's him. I just blocked his access. He's not even allowed to use this system. How would a beat cop know about this other than what they're allowed to see on their cruiser scanners? Can you pull his file for me please?" he said. Vince was not only the IT expert for the department, but he was also a police officer. A kind of 'plain clothes' officer. When he'd first been offered the IT security position, he took advantage of a then existing program where he could go to the academy and become a county officer as an option. He'd realized four weeks into it he didn't want to be a beat cop, patrolman—whatever. But he finished and received his commission, then assumed his department IT position. He looked like a Teamsters enforcer —and talked like one, too. He was big and muscular, but as friendly a man as you'd ever meet. Unless you tread on his system, that is. That was his baby. He took it as a personal affront that anyone could get by him.

"Here you go, handsome." Shelby plopped Whitman's file on his desk in front of him. Vince looked at her and smiled.

"You ever comb your hair?" he said. She stuck her tongue out at him and he laughed.

"I can't do anything with it. It's crazy, isn't it?" she said.

"It looks great. It suits you too. I was pulling your leg," he said. She looked behind her at her station desk. Then sat down in the wheely chair.

"Do you need to go back to your post? I can come out and see you in a few minutes, and let you know what I've found?" he said.

"Naah, I'll wait. It's still early. If anyone comes in, I'll run out there," she said. Vince started into the file. After turning a page or two, he saw something. He started flipping through faster, looking for auxiliary documents. Then stopped and turned to the system, typing commands and instructions.

"He's been looking for address and phone numbers of Phoebe Rinnder and the ex-wife of Rick Cameron along with any of their addresses, past and present. He's successfully accessed and pulled them out of deep security in the FBI leg of the system. Red, who's Rick Cameron?" he said. Shelby Gallagher put both her hands up to her mouth.

"Talk to me Red. Can you get someone to cover your desk for a few minutes?" he said. She jumped up and ran over to admin and asked her friend Gail Chmura if she could sit up front for ten minutes.

"Glad to love. I'm tired of standing right now, anyway. Take as long as you need," Gail said. Gallagher sat back down with Vince and started in. She explained to him Cameron was a former police officer terminated for cause. A record of excessive force along with other questionable rule and protocol violations.

"And get this, it wasn't on public record, but his wife divorced him for physical abuse. I heard it through the grapevine he did a number on her. Several times. A real piece of work. I was glad when the department deep-sixed him," she said. Vince cringed at the idea of a man physically beating a woman. Working at the police department, he knew it happened more than people thought. But it got him in the gut every time he heard about it.

"They didn't arrest him in the process of his investigation?" he said.

"Someone did him a 'favor.' It's impossible to know who it was—probably a retired senior member of the force. Who knows? I wish they'd put his ass in prison though," she said.

"Wait. I found something. Look at this; Whitman has IT experience. He'd even started training on this system once. It was before I was on board. They pulled him for some reason and he stayed on as a regular officer. Someone must've seen a chink in his armor or a character flaw and he got yanked. That's how he knows how to maneuver around in here. Not anymore though," he said.

"How will you catch him?" she said. Vince turned and looked at Gallagher. He nodded and pointed at her.

"Gallagher, good point. I got a better idea," he said. Vince started typing commands and looking at the screen. The keyboard clicking away as he did. Shelby sat watching.

"I set a 'trap.' When he logs in again, it'll capture the details of his login and name, who he is and what he was looking for, then lock up. He won't be able to cover his tracks because I've made it so, as far as he's concerned, the system will be frozen. I'll be notified the second it happens and will have him detained. It's a terminable offense, too," he said.

"What about the stuff he already pulled from the system?" she said.

"Yeah. That's what pisses me more than anything right now. It's too late to have stopped that, and he's surely already given that to Cameron. But why?" he said. Vince sat, thinking. Tapping one end of a pencil on the desk, rotating it and tapping and repeating. He dropped the pencil onto the desk and spun around towards Shelby.

"Whitman's guilty of a security violation as an unauthorized user of the system. It's grounds for termination, but it's the lesser of much bigger potential problems. Cameron's still out there. Why? Why is Whitman risking his career for Cameron? We need to find out," he said.

Roy Whitman started smoking again. He'd already started smoking on and off after the shooting a few years back. Not initially, but after a couple weeks when he'd considered the way the scenario played out that day after he shot and killed Roderigo Gaston. It wasn't so much the shooting but the underhanded way he and Rick Cameron reported the incident. And how Rick Cameron 'set him up.' He believed Cameron was trying to help him—in his own way. What he considered 'helping,' that is. It was a nightmare for Whitman. Then the visit from Cameron recently and his demands, with the implicit threat of exposing the events from the shooting long ago. Whitman knew he was in deep already and thought about just going straight to Sergeant Jamison the same afternoon Cameron dropped by his house. And tell him about the shooting and what actually happened with Gaston. Now he'd dug himself in so deep, having also breached the security of the Henrico County Police Department, retrieving information without authorization, not to mention unauthorized operation and access of the system. A federal crime now. And even worse than any of that, providing Cameron information he should well have known could be to the hurt of someone. So it was almost three packs a day now. Plus, he was careless and'd even been spotted several times smoking in uniform while on duty.

"I don't care anymore," he thought. Cameron told him to get one more thing. Addresses and phone numbers of Samuel Rinnder, his ex-wife's father.

"This is the last thing I'm getting for you Cam," he said.

"Whitman, I'll let you know when it's the last thing, understand?" Cameron said.

"Yeah, sure Rick," he said. Cameron knew Whitman was wearying of his demands. That he'd probably have to make do with what he had after this.

"I won't need him anymore after this anyway," he thought.

Work was progressing beautifully on the toll road segment. Mike and his crew were closing the gap on delays they'd had working on it. An improvement, not complete closure. Still a good feeling, though. Milton Cross was happy, which meant the company was happy. Which means Kiewit would almost surely receive the contracts for the next two sections of road. Mike stood by his truck, having just gotten off the phone with Cross.

"We getting the next section?" Ray asked him.

"You know they never come out and say it. At least not at this stage. But reading between the lines, I think so, Ray. It's not inked yet and not official—my opinion only. So don't spread it around yet, ok?" he said. Ray nodded. He was still happy, though. The idea of staying in the same area another year or more on the same basic project was good for him.

"I'll keep it under my hat," he said.

"You can tell Bruno, but let him know the same thing, to keep quiet about it for a little while. I'll let you two know when it's final," Mike said. He stood by his truck, looking over the site plans. Again. He was always looking for the 'little' things that could cause problems later. He took a drink of his coffee and thought about what a great time he'd had with Gavin. The visit and the hunting. He'd gone out both Sundays with his brother. Gavin didn't expect him to go twice. Mike considered it an 'investment.' The early mornings were a small price to know he'd spent that time with his brother when he had the opportunity. That first Sunday after their pizza dinner and Ruth's Chris Saturday night, they'd each gotten a good sized buck.

"You did it again," Gavin said. Mike'd waited and considered the terrain, high bark abrasions on trees near a clearing. Also, the way the mountain sloped and where he'd expect the deer to be moving. At one point that morning,

Gavin was getting ready to take a buck he saw after they'd been set for over an hour. Gavin was taking aim when he felt the barrel of his gun move up. He looked up and Mike gently urged him to wait. Not to take the shot. 'Open season' didn't mean unlimited on bucks; only one per day. Unlimited for does. He looked up at Mike, who had his finger to his lips. Then he held a finger in the air. He meant wait. Gavin nodded. Sure enough, not even two minutes later, buck one made his was through the clearing and here came buck two. Twice as many points. Gavin pursed his lips as if he was whistling, glanced up at his brother, then set up to take the shot. Not as easy either with black powder; it's a slow-moving projectile and sometimes the buck would bolt before it 'arrived.'

They both got one each for the day. The second Sunday was more about being out together. Mike made as if he would hunt, getting his brother's second rifle ready. He just wanted to be with Gavin while he could. Neither of them took a shot. Gavin could have but set the gun down and sat up. Mike was already sitting nearby.

"Beautiful out here, isn't it?" Gavin said. Mike nodded. They cleaned up and headed home.

"You ever shoot that 300 Win Mag rifle I gave you a few years ago?" Gavin said. It was later that Sunday back at the house. They put everything up and were going inside to have something to eat. His brother was referring to the Winchester Model 70 scoped hunting rifle he'd given Mike for his 50th a couple of years earlier.

"Brother, I've never taken it out. I'm sorry, man. Rifle season for deer is only three days long. I never seem to have the opportunity to get out when the season's open," he said.

"Maybe when you retire," he said. He knew in Mike's work he was under constant pressure almost all the time. He was glad they paid him well for the trouble. If he lived long enough, he'd be able to take it easy down the road.

"Yeah, maybe then," he said.

"I sighted that thing in myself before I sent it to you. It's spot on at a hundred and fifty yards. You go hunting with that you won't be able to miss," he said.

It'd been over a week now since Gavin left and went back home to Rhode Island. Mike relished the time and was thankful he went out with him. It was a great time together, where they now both have a wonderful memory of time well spent. Mike stood by the back of his truck at the site and sighed. He was glad for the work he had and loved it. There just wasn't much of a breather most of the time. He was first there today.

"Ray will be here shortly," he said. He loved the guys and knew once they showed and they started work for the day, he'd be happy.

"Good for the soul. Work." It's what his father'd tell him.

Chapter 8

The Super24 was hopping already. It wasn't even six-thirty in the morning and it was hard to park or pull out because there were so many cars coming and going. Mike Netherland backed into a spot with his white Silverado. He'd finished a call with Bruno and when he was in process of stepping out to go get a coffee, his phone rang.

"It's Milt," he said. Looking at the phone. He half sat back in the truck to take the call. It was brief and had to do with a signature release on a Caterpillar crane the company'd been using at the job.

"Make sure you sign off at the end of the day today with the lease crewman. Take a picture of the document and send it to me," he said.

"Will do Milt. I understand—we want them to know we're finished with it today," he said. Mike nodded and jotted down a note on the pad clipped to his contractor clipboard. Milt was prattling on a moment about charges or something when Mike saw a gray Volvo S40 station wagon pull in and he recognized the trim brunette with short hair in the passenger seat.

"Yeah, I understand Milt. I'll definitely sign the release and put the time on it like you said. We're trying to keep costs contained. But hey look, I gotta run. The guys are waiting for me to bring coffees to the site. I'll send you the picture of the signed document before we close down the site tonight," he said. The brunette he'd 'met' in the Super24 a few weeks ago was sitting in the car. A woman got out of the driver's side and headed in. She looked about the same age as his 'friend.' He got out of the truck and headed into the Super24, walking around the driver's side. He tried to be discrete and look behind him casually.

"She's resting," he thought. Her eyes were closed, and she was laying back on the seat. He got three medium cups of dark roast, threw a bunch of little creamer tubs, fifteen packets of sugar, and some stirring sticks into the center area of the cup holder. Making haste, he snapped three lids on the cups and stood looking around. He spotted the woman who he was sure had to be related to her passenger. She had a similar face, but was a little more solidly built. Not heavy, but solid. Her hair was light brown.

"She's got to be the sister." He thought. She had two coffees in her hands and was looking over the fresh breakfast sandwiches and picked up two of them. Mike positioned himself to get in line in front of her, but kind of standing by. When he thought she was about to pay, he got in line first. Then she did an about face and looked at the sandwiches again, as if she was going to change her mind. By the time she got in line, someone was between her and Mike.

"Ahh, forget it," he thought. Mike focused on just getting out of the store and was next up. The person who was between him and the woman stepped out of line. Remembering they'd forgotten something now. Mike placed his coffees down.

"Morning," Mike said to the cashier.

"Good morning. Are the coffees it?" the cashier said.

"No, I'll get her stuff too," he said. Gesturing to the woman.

"Oh, that's not necessary. Thanks though," she said.

"I insist. Someone did me a favor earlier and I'm in a good mood. Please, ok?" he said.

"What can I say? I'm not going to argue about a free breakfast, right?" she said, smiling. Mike was good natured and pleasant. People usually liked him, so Phoebe let him pay.

"There you go. Have a good day then," he said.

"You too. Thank you so much," she said. Mike made as if he was bolting out, then turned to the woman.

"I'm Mike," he said.

"Mike, nice to meet you. Phoebe. You're very nice. Thanks again, and have a good day," she said.

"You too Phoebe," he said. Without lingering, Mike made a beeline to his truck. Phoebe lingered a moment, getting some pepper packets from the condiment stand, then went out. She'd just caught Mike getting into his truck and closing the door. She opened the handle on the car and her sister woke up. Startled.

"Hey, she said. I must've fallen asleep. Sorry Phoebe," she said.

"Rest all you want. I didn't get any sleep last night either, so I don't blame you," she said. Phoebe wanted to start a diatribe against her poor sister's ex, who'd been calling them now on her work, home and cell phones. But she refrained, knowing she'd just upset her sister plus probably start swearing like a drunken sailor.

"A friendly guy in the store bought this for us. His good deed for the day, I guess. He was in front of me in line and picked up the tab. That's him back there in the white truck. Nice guy too. He said his name's Mike," she said. Her sister turned to look behind her and did a double take. Phoebe noticed her reaction.

"Do you know him?" she said.

"No. I mean, not really. I ran into him here a couple of weeks ago when I was getting a coffee," she said.

"Good-looking guy. Seems nice too," she said. Her sister turned back around to the front and shrugged.

"I know. The weight of the world's on your shoulders. Mine too," she said. Phoebe turned around again and looked back at Mike in his truck. He'd just put it in gear when he saw her. He tipped his hat lightly to her and started out.

"Thanks for getting the coffee and sandwich, Phoebe. And our friend too, I guess, right?" she said. They started eating and sat there chatting over coffee. Phoebe had to keep fighting the urge to verbally lay into her sister's ex, but tried to remind herself it wouldn't do any good. He was still 'out there.' She wished he was dead. She hated the idea of wishing anyone was dead, but thought if anyone deserved it, he'd be a fine candidate. They finished up and were sitting quietly. A pall over their visit. Phoebe was still glad they were together. After they finished up, Phoebe drove the two of them back home.

"Another quiet day at the house," she thought. "Hostages in my own home. 'Courtesy' of that human debris, Rick Cameron," she thought.

Rick Cameron fumed about being an outsider now. No access anymore to the police records system. He had leverage over Whitman, but knew that was ending. Plus, he'd come to the realization anything he did to implicate Whitman would also come back to bite him. He had more than enough information to find his wife now, anyway. Her new name, her address in Atlanta, and that she was visiting her sister here in Virginia. All he needed now was her father's address and phone numbers, and he'd have everything he 'needed.'

"The old man'd gotten his info taken off public record, too. Along with all new unlisted phone numbers. I'll go see him in due time," he thought. He walked around the warehouse in the dark, wishing his shift was over. After he'd gotten some rest when he went home, he planned to take a drive.

"Ok bitch. Your phone's off—I'll come see you personally," he said. He was walking his 'beat.' Rick Cameron would've been happy if someone trespassed here tonight.

Roy Whitman's wife knew he was in trouble. Roy was a pretty good man. He didn't have poor character exactly. He wanted to do right, but allowed himself to take shortcuts, and because he didn't maintain his position on higher ground, he'd set himself up for a fall.

"Honey, I know something's bothering you. I've asked you, but you won't tell me what it is. You're not just smoking again, but you're sweating a lot. Like you're under a great stress. Before you go to work, do you want to talk to me?" she said.

"I'd like to Pamela. And I will soon. Tonight. This is the last time. This morning is it, then I'm through. I'll be fine then and we can talk," he said.

"The last time for what, Roy?" she said.

"Someone's pressuring me to get some information for them from the work database. I'm going to help one last time today, then I'm through," he said.

"Is that allowed, Roy?" she said.

"No, of course not. I'm just doing him a favor. But today's the last time," he said.

"Why don't you stop now? Don't get it for him. Tell your Sergeant and get it over with before it gets any worse,' she said.

"It can't get any worse than it is now," he said. Almost yelling. He was sorry he'd raised his voice at his wife. She stopped and left it alone but told him she hoped everything would be ok. But she couldn't hide her concern for him and wondered why her husband was doing a 'favor' for someone. She was sure it wasn't out of goodwill, but knew if she pressed him anymore, he'd clam up even worse. Roy made his way to the precinct. It was early and before his shift started. So he could get in, then head to out to his designated patrol area for the day. He was surprised to see Shelby Gallagher in already.

"Maybe they adjusted her desk duty," he thought. They were sure whoever was accessing the system, and were pretty much convinced it was Whitman, would do so again in the next two weeks. As a favor to Vince, Shelby agreed to come in an hour early for the next three weeks. He'd gotten permission for her to have two paid days off she could use, like regular leave for helping. She would've done it gratis for him, but didn't complain about the two days. This was only the second day. She never chatted much with staff when they came and went. Gallagher was cordial but not really interested in a lot of chit-chat with everyone. It wasn't personal, but it took an hour for her first coffee of the day to start 'working.' Plus, she had minimal tolerance for a lot of people, other than those few on her 'short list.' Like Vince Romano and a couple of her other girlfriends who worked in admin. Roy gave her a peremptory hello and headed into the building. Gallagher surreptitiously looked towards him over her shoulder. The doors to the security system were right behind her, just inside the main glass double doors.

"He walked right past them," she thought. It was a ruse. Every so often, she'd look over her shoulder again. From where she sat, it wasn't easy from inside to see if she was looking. She could notice if the doors to the secure area were being opened but not be seen by someone going in. Here, she saw Roy had doubled back, then went in. She was just curious since she knew there was active monitoring in progress so anyone entering and leaving was being 'watched' by an assigned officer who was to alert Vince along with an IAD uniformed officer.

"The shit's gonna hit the fan now," Shelby said. She had

nothing against Whitman personally except that he was helping a known wife beater ex cop. Vince also hinted to her they'd discovered a previously cleared but questionable shooting incident that might have something to do with why he was doing this.

"It's incredibly stupid that he honestly thinks he could get away with this," he said. It was Gabe Whelan. A uniformed IAD officer few people knew was in IAD. He reported to Sharon Wilder and was assisting Vince Romano. Romano was watching a screen intently and saw that Whitman logged in. The trap Romano'd set was next. And now they'd know exactly what data he was getting.

"Samuel Rinnder. Who's that?" Vince said under his breath.

"The Dad. Good night. Ok Whelan, he's in and the trap springs… now," he said. On a video feed Vince and Gabe Whelan were watching and you could see Whitman frantically typing keys and looking at the screen. He stood, then sat down to try again.

"Go get him," Whelan said. He was talking into a police radio, instructing two officers assigned to apprehend Whitman.

"If we can get to Cameron through this guy, it would be good. Better late than never," he said. Still galled, though, someone somewhere called in a favor to help him when he was found guilty by IAD of multiple counts of police brutality.

The phone rang at the front desk.

"Shelby Gallagher." It was an inside call, so she used her name. Outside calls were 'Henrico County Police, may I help you?'

"It was him. We got him. Sit tight, beautiful—they're coming to get him now," Vince said.

"Hey Vince. Thanks for calling and letting me know. Maybe we can talk about it tonight over a coffee. Or even dinner?" she said. There was silence.

"Vince?' she said.

"It's a department phone—they can hear personal stuff," he said.

"So," she said. He laughed.

"Yes," he said.

"Yes, what?' she said.

"It's a date. Gotta go Red," he said. Gallagher formed her lips as if she was giving a kiss but didn't make any sound.

"See you later, big boy."

Chapter 9

Rick Cameron could never reach Royland Whitman again. The reason is Henrico County Police confiscated his 'special' phone when they placed him under arrest. And every time Cameron called the number, he heard a bunch of clicks, then a beep sound, which went into silence. After several attempts over a few day period he realized his number was almost certainly being captured, including any words he spoke into the phone.

"Too late now for me to do anything about that. I never said more than 'hello' and 'Roy, are you there?' So they have nothing on me," he thought. He removed the chip from the phone and bent it back and forth until it cracked and threw the halves away, then tossed the phone itself into a sewer drain.

"They probably caught him. I should've stopped pushing before," he said. Talking out loud to himself. It was true enough, too. Whitman was arrested, and the department figured everything out. He sang like a bird and confessed in tears how the shooting'd gone awry and Cameron was backup and covered for him. He spilled his guts, knowing they'd be able to put the pieces together anyway by close examination of the old case file of the shooting. Whitman was glad. At least that they caught him. Unfortunately, the bigger problem was the information he'd provided to Cameron would or could be used to hurt someone. That still ate him and it would do him little good if he 'cooperated' now that they had caught him. The entire department was against him. There was no goodwill anywhere other than his wife. And that wouldn't keep him out of prison. Sharon Wilder herself, usually very level, was furious and set to make an example of Whitman. Also making it clear to the entire force if she even thought someone was protecting Whitman or Cameron anymore, she'd report the incident to the Mayor, the Virginia State Senator for their district, and the Congressional Law Enforcement oversight committee for internal affairs case tampering. She met with Captain Mattias and had a quiet but very pointed meeting emphasizing to him he could have overridden the 'favor' granted to Cameron those years ago.

"And Captain, I understand I report to you—officially. But only in so far as you support IAD. You understand, right?" Polite, but making it crystal clear there'd be no more favors.

"Sharon, I understand. You're tough as hell. And I want a clean force here too. I mean it and wish we could go back and undo all that. Right now, I want you to know I'll support whatever we need to do," he said.

"Good. Very good. Because I'm going to throw the book at Whitman, and if I figure out a way to do it, I'm looking for a way to take Cameron off the street. I'm doing you a favor, too. You don't want these characters on your watch. At least I hope you don't," she said. She stood, not waiting for an answer, and left his office. Mattias sat at his desk, tapping a pencil on his desk for a moment.

"Whew. I wouldn't want her after me," he said. Mattias was horrified too that Whitman, by his actions, will have enabled that menace Cameron. It was a nightmare scenario which could also bring him down. His own sergeants weren't supportive of him giving the break to Cameron before. He had no more cover.

"It would just be easier to go shoot the bastard myself," he thought. He shook his head, stood up, and told his secretary to call a meeting of all his sergeants in thirty minutes.

Rick Cameron drove over to Phoebe Rinnder's neighborhood, going through a side street to get where he could see the house, but far enough away he wouldn't be noticed. He did a double take when he saw an unmarked police car parked on the street near the house.

"What the hell? What's a cruiser doing here?" he thought.

"Whitman. That's gotta be it," he said. He sat in the car thinking.

"They wouldn't be here if they weren't keeping an eye out for me." Wondering what he'd do now. He'd gotten off his shift less than two hours ago, so it was still early. His plan was to come and pay the girls a 'visit.' Fuming now over the poor turn his life had taken and now this. He felt his coat pocket. He had his 'off duty' gun on him. A smooth barrel revolver. No way ballistics could be traced back to it. He wished now he'd capped the both of them that day he followed Phoebe on her shopping trip.

"It would've been easy then," he thought. He started up, about to leave, and saw his ex driving out in her own car. The cruiser wasn't moving, and he decided he'd see if he could follow her discretely.

"Here we go," he said. Traffic was light, which made it easier to tail someone from a distance. His ex was smart but wouldn't likely consider someone would follow her. She pulled into the Super24 parking lot, which she was relieved to see was busy.

The officer assigned to Phoebe's house in the car outside spoke to her and her sister early that morning and explained enough details of the situation so they were aware there was some danger.

"Tell me about it. The asshole cornered me at CVS a few days ago. So he's been here already. Not that I'm ungrateful for the help. But it's always the same. The police show up at the same time as the hearse," she said. It was Phoebe. The officer tried not to smile. He hated that it always seemed like it was so often the case.

"I know how you feel, but I'm here. And I don't make the rules. He's a genuine piece of work, though; I know that," he said. Phoebe nodded, but was still irked.

"Officer, I appreciate the help. I don't know how much good it'll be. He's a smart and malicious man. But I know it's what it is," she said. It was Cameron's former wife, no longer a 'Cameron.' Unfortunately, her ex got all the information he needed from Whitman already. The officer didn't say they couldn't leave the house but that 'he recommended' they don't. He'd been told enough to know the guy was a very bad apple; the worst, in fact. But because of past decisions they'd made at the Henrico County Police Department, they couldn't put out an arrest warrant for him on actions he'd previously been 'cleared' of when he was terminated. They could try to do it, but it would cause a lot of damage to the department because an outside investigation would ensue as to why Cameron was allowed to 'skate' before. Which is why Wilder read the riot act to Mattias and anyone else that she thought might decide to resist her current efforts.

"I've warned you all. Don't get in my way. Even better, give me a hand, if you know what's good for you," she said. She was furious and would bring down anyone that helped Cameron or Whitman escape her wrath. She wasn't out of control either; and that's what was scary. Sharon Wilder knew every law, all procedural violations, and police behavioral requirements. She'd make a case so tight a duck's ass would seem loose.

Cameron was able to follow his ex easily in the light morning traffic and, from as far back as he was, saw her pull into the Super24. Driving past the first entrance, he went in at the next drive, parking on the opposite side of the store. He was sure his ex would've been happy the place was hopping. He was too. It was even easier to stay 'unnoticed' if you knew what you were doing when a place was crowded and busy. He walked around the outside of the store the long way, where they brought in deliveries.

"Now's the tricky part," he thought. Getting close enough to her car without her seeing him first. Standing close to the store wall, Cameron acting as nonchalantly as he could. He watched and waited for a few minutes; and knew she didn't linger when she went into a store. Then he saw the car lights blink and could 'hear' his ex-wife's walk as she made her way to the car. At that same moment, Mike Netherland, who'd backed into his usual spot earlier, saw her coming out and heading to the car. He was making calls and looking at paperwork on his clipboard and didn't notice her when she first arrived. He'd also never seen her in a car except the time she was with her friend—or sister—not too long ago.

"Georgia?" he said. Netherland was looking at the license plate on her car and saw the distinct orange peach underneath her plate number.

"She's from Georgia?" he thought. Then he noticed the fast opening of her passenger side door and a burly-looking man hopping inside right after she got in. The man closed the door immediately and looked towards her. He could see his 'friend' was startled and scared. She started to get out, and Mike saw the man grab her arm and restrain her.

"Sit still and shut up, bitch. I'll shoot you right here if you try to get out," he said. He held her arm in a police grip that prevented her from getting away. Mike stepped out of his truck and made his way over to the passenger side of her car.

A light green Ford Fusion. He knew a woman in trouble when he saw it. What he was about to do depended on the door being unlocked.

"Let go of me Cam, you're hurting me," she said.

"I spent a long time looking for you and—" The passenger door opened and Mike half grabbed, half acted as if he was greeting an old friend.

"Hey, everybody ok in here?" he said.

"Get your hands off me. Who the hell are you anyway?" Cameron said. Taking the revolver out of his pocket and turning it towards Mike.

"Watch out. He's got a gun," she said. He was sure he was going for a gun before Cameron had even gotten it out of his pocket. Mike grabbed his wrist and turned it so Rick Cameron couldn't hold the gun properly.

"I wouldn't do that, friend," Mike said. Cameron had no choice but to let go of his ex-wife and she jumped out of the car and scanned the parking lot for a police car. Then ran into the store and asked the manager to call the police.

"My ex-husband is outside and has a gun," she said. Mike twisted Cameron's wrist so far he knew it was right on the cusp of breaking.

"The guy's strong," Mike thought.

"Pardner, you better let go of that gun or I'm breakin' your wrist—right now. Cameron stood to reduce the leverage Mike had and let the gun go. It clattered to the pavement.

"I'm a cop, you asshole," he said.

"No, you're not. And if you are, you won't be for long," Mike said. He continued to hold his wrist and positioned himself to wrap his free arm around his back and pull him to the ground. He could tell the guy knew how to hurt someone.

"Let me go," Cameron said.

"I'll let you go when I'm ready. You try anything in my space and I'm taking you down. And don't even think about bending down to get the gun," he said. Two Henrico County Police cruisers drove in, pulling up behind the two of them. Mike let him go and stayed ready.

"Next time, you won't have the upper hand. I'll make sure of it," Cameron said in a low voice.

"We'll see," Netherland said. Cameron looked towards the ground and knew he wouldn't have a chance reaching for the gun and started walking.

"Hold on a minute, I need to speak with you," one officer said. Cameron half ignored him but stopped to avoid an arrest for 'running.'

"Someone called and said a man had a gun. Was that either of you?" He said.

"It wasn't me. That gentleman had a gun, which he dropped," Mike said.

"I own it legally and forgot I had it in my coat pocket. I was having a talk with this man and we were done. Unless you have a reason to take me in, I'm leaving. Anything else?" he said.

"Where's the gun the woman called about?"

"Owning a gun is not a crime. Like I said, I forgot I had it on me. I'm leaving now unless I've done something that is grounds for an arrest," he said. He started walking towards his vehicle on the other side of the store. Cameron knew the law, police protocol, and procedure. The young officers that arrived didn't know who he was—which probably helped him. One of them followed him from a distance and watched him get into his car. He was wearing the new body cams which were on, so the vehicle and the plate were recorded. Cameron gave a peremptory wave towards the officer. A 'See you, have a good day officer' wave. The officer shook his head and went back to Netherland. He'd told the officers the guy was restraining a woman in her car. He opened the door to help her and the guy inside pulled out a gun, which he dropped.

"It's under the car," Mike said.

"I opened the door to interrupt because it looked like it was getting out of hand," he added. He also apologized for foisting himself onto what may have been just a bad domestic squabble. The one officer who'd gotten the scan went over to his squad car and put in the plate number. He'd jotted it down on a pad when he walked back.

The screen popped up 'Richard Cameron' and all his pertinents, how he was a former police officer, his current address, vehicles and a few other things. There were different codes on the screen only certain people could access, which would reveal more information. It was enough for now. He walked over to the other officer who was trying to decide whether to bring Mike in for questioning.

"I'm happy to go in, officer, if you need me to. I was hoping—"

"Leave it alone, man. Let him go; that was Cameron," the one officer said.

"Mr. Netherland, just a minute please," he said. The two officers stepped aside and were talking. The one that was talking with Mike started nodding. He turned back to Mike and asked if he knew the woman who was in the car.

"I've seen her around a couple of times, otherwise I don't know her. I would've done the same for any troubled woman; it's what my father taught me," he said.

"Ok, Mr. Netherland. Thanks so much. Call us if any time if you need to. We have your number too and if we need anything else, we'll call you," he said. Mike shook his hand. The officer'd already picked up the gun with gloves, emptying the rounds into a separate evidence bag. Mike saw him look down the barrel after he'd taken the rounds out.

"Look at this," he said. Showing another officer the bore.

"It's smooth. A replacement barrel?" he said. The one nodded and put the gun in an evidence bag.

"Mr. Netherland, thanks again. Sorry for all the trouble. When we show up, we don't know who's done what. Who's good, bad. So we assume everyone is." he said.

"I know the drill. And understand," Mike said. The two officers headed into the Super24 to see the woman.

Chapter 10

"That was my ex-husband, Rick Cameron. He must've followed me here today, and I didn't realize it. We divorced several years ago and because of his record of abuse and violence, I assumed a new identity and also moved out of state. How he got my phone number I don't know. Both my home and cell," she said. One officer with her received a call from Sergeant Jamison and stepped aside.

"We're talking to the ex-wife now. Former Mrs. Cameron," he said. And explained they were questioning her about what happened.

"Don't be stupid. The woman's not guilty, do you understand? The problem is Rick Cameron. Keep it in mind, ok?" he said.

"Yes Sir, I understand," he said. The point was, don't grill the poor woman. Help her out. He returned to the woman who was talking with the other officer.

"I'm up here visiting my sister in Virginia and he has her address, too. He won't leave me alone; either of us. I don't really know the man outside, but am certainly glad he helped me today. I'd said hello to him once in the store and I've bumped into him here a time or two. And once when I was here with my sister getting a coffee. That's it. And last I knew, it's still a free country. I thought it was ok to be friendly to people," she said.

"Yes Ma'am. We just need to know what the relationships are. If we—"

"If you'd cared about people, you wouldn't've enabled a thug like Rick Cameron to be out walking the streets. My relationships are none of your business either, and I haven't done a damn thing. Rick Cameron is a dangerous man. More than you know. You could've put him away and you didn't. Now he's after me. I'm sure you'll be very sorry when you show up to take the evidence pictures after he kills me. Don't you people have any foresight at all?" she said. There wasn't much they could say. The one who'd just gotten off the phone with Jamison nodded lightly. He knew she had a point. It's the way it usually was; the police weren't able to do jack to stop a crime. It would be like preemptively arresting a person before they'd done anything. All he knew was Jamison and IAD wanted Cameron.

"We're working to see if we can't pull a rabbit out of our hats here and arrest the asshole for something that'll stick," Jamison said, just before he'd hung up.

The officers thanked Cameron's ex and exchanged cards.

"I know the routine. 'Call if I have anything for you.' And don't bother calling me on my phone. It's off. I can't even enjoy this visit with my sister with him out there. I know you have your hands tied behind your back. You can't go shoot him or you'd be just like him. But as long as he's on the streets, I have no peace at all. None," she said.

The police walked out of the Super24 and Mike sat waiting in his truck.

"Bruno, thanks for covering for me. I'll be up to the site shortly," he said.

"Glad to help Mike. You should've capped his ass when

you had the chance. Probably what I would've done."

"The old west—I know. It was easier then. Not so much now, though. You know, arrests, prosecutions, and court cases. You might've heard of those things."

"I might've. But it probably wouldn't've stopped me. Glad you're ok though, Mike."

"Thanks Bruno. See you in fifteen."

"Mike, don't forget some coffees before you come up. We're dying up here of withdrawal."

"Yeah, yeah. I got you," he said. The woman was looking around by her car, about to get in. Mike hopped out of the cab as she was getting inside.

"Hey Georgia," he hollered. She hesitated a minute.

"Georgia," he said. He started walking over. She turned to look and saw Mike coming. He kept his distance, and she turned to him in her seat.

"I know you're not ok so I won't say 'I hope you are.' Is there anything I can do to help you?" he said.

"You already did. And I appreciate it. He would've killed me. And I'm sorry to tell you, but you're guaranteed to be on his shit list now. He'll be looking for you." Mike was quiet.

"Lady, you want a coffee? I'm getting some for my crew and myself," he said.

"Not today, thank you. You better take care of yourself," she said. A wan expression on her face.

"Sure. You do the same," he said. Mike tipped his hat to her, and she closed the door. When he walked inside the store, she sighed heavily. She'd let Phoebe vent today all she wanted.

"Hell, I'll even join in myself," she said. There were no tears when she drove away. Dry pain was all that was there. It seemed now Henrico's finest decided to post a twenty-four hour watch at Phoebe's house.

"They're trying. Finally," she said to herself. More hope in her words than any realistic expectation.

Mike put the tray of coffees in the cab and climbed up onto the back of his truck. He had one of those large heavy duty locking tool boxes on the back. He unlocked it and opened the lid. Inside were some company surveying instruments he used for road engineering projects. He removed them and set them down on the truck bed. He moved a few items around, including some wool work blankets, and saw what he was looking for. It'd been a few years, and he didn't remember if it was still in the truck. It was a leather case with a characteristic shape. He unzipped it and pulled it apart. He knelt down and looked inside and read the markings on the side. 'Winchester Model 70 – New Haven Connecticut – .300 Win Mag.' A straight 4x power Leupold scope mounted on the gun. It looked like new. Still gleaming from the light coating of gun oil Gavin'd treated the gun with before he gave it to Mike. He felt around inside the case.

"Here they are," he said. He pulled out two boxes of factory new Winchester brand 300 Win Mag ammo. All of it—gun, scope and ammo, courtesy of his brother. Mike shook his head. Like he was shaking water out of his ears.

"What am I doing?" he thought. He put the ammo boxes back inside and zipped up the case. He covered it all up carefully and put the instruments back in the toolbox and locked it up. In the cab driving to the site, he shook his head again. Like trying to make a bad dream or memory go away. But it wouldn't.

"That's crazy Mike. Don't even think about it," he said. As he drove up the highway, he started shaking. He'd dealt with some rotten apples in his life, but this guy scared him. He remembered a story his father'd told him as he drove up. It was long ago, when Mike was still in junior high. An incident where a bully threatened Mike at school. He was getting good at varsity wrestling and told Gavin he'd fix the kid's ass good on the playground the next day. He'd tripped a heavyset girl in the hallway and Mike saw him do it. The 'bully' stood laughing. Mike helped the girl up, who was crying uncontrollably. She wasn't hurt, but badly humiliated. He turned and looked at the laughing bully. John Demonte. A chunky, mean spirited punk kid. The kid's whole family were either already criminals, future criminals, or already behind bars. Mike glared at him that day after he'd helped the girl.

"You don't like it Mikey? Tough," he said.

"We'll see tomorrow. After lunch," Mike said.

"Yeah. I'll be ready and you'll be sorry too," he said. Then walked off. At home, he told his brother Gavin he'd 'fix Demonte' during recess break after lunch. Dad heard him from in the hallway and told him he wanted to talk with him. In the kitchen.

"Can I come too Dad?" Gavin said.

"Sure you can. Let's all three of us go sit down," he said.

"Michael, Gavin—this is from almost fourteen years ago and I've never told you before. If either of you boys have questions as I tell you, I want you to ask me. Ok?" he said.

"Yeah, sure Dad," they both said.

"An incident occurred to me once too; a long while ago now. A man I knew down at the supply depot cornered your mother and put his hands on her in a way that, to me, suggested rape. And I can tell you now, after these many years, his behavior was wrong. Dead wrong, and was an offense to me, your mother, and I'm sure to God, too. Mom was all shook up, and I was furious. She begged me to leave it alone. Or just call the police and file a report. Did I do it? I was a fool. I went down there and found him and beat the hell out of him. He didn't resist. Afterwards I was sick I did it. I broke some of his bones, and two of his teeth were so badly damaged they had to be removed. You boys with me so far?" he said. They nodded. Completely silent.

"Now, I was the one arrested. The man, who you don't know, didn't want me to be. He told me how sorry he was for touching Mom. The police were called by the supply depot manager and they had no choice but to arrest me for assault and battery. And this is the punchline I want you boys to understand. I not only didn't make your mother proud, but I did her and you little guys more harm than good. I got convicted on a reduced sentence and was a shame to your Momma and to myself. The guy was wrong. But I could have talked with him man to man. Maybe gotten a witness and ask him to apologize to her. I could have called the police. I know the police can't stop someone if they're not there. But I could have made a point that way. Maybe he would have been cited for offensive behavior, or something else just to teach him a lesson. It's been a while now, but I tell you to this day I wish I'd never done it. He was a bit of a rogue. But not as bad as a lot of other men I've known. Usually the worse men will destroy themselves, anyway. You don't need to do it for them," he said. Finishing the story.

Mike started to calm, thinking about that day his father talked to him and Gavin.

"Like a real life Leave it to Beaver episode. Only a real man, in both ways, telling the story," he thought. He took a big pull of his coffee, which he'd added plenty of cream and sugar to.

"Boy, that's good for the nerves," he said. He looked at his hand, which he held out in front of him after setting the coffee down.

"Still shaky, but getting better," he thought.

"That thing goes back in the house. Tonight," he said. Kiewit didn't mind limited personal use of their vehicles and he had hoped to get out hunting at some point. But he didn't want the rifle in the truck anymore. Not right now.

"Dad's right," he thought. He hopped out of the truck with the tray of coffees, his already half gone.

"Mike, man, I'm about to have a seizure from withdrawal. What kept you?" Ray said.

"Here's your coffee. You're not gonna believe what just happened," he said. He told Ray the story. Bruno came over to get his coffee, who he'd already given the summary version of events to on the phone. He showed the guys the cards from the police officers.

"I would've shot the dirt bag right then. Or at least made sure he had a good memory about his actions," Ray said.

"Yeah, maybe. The guy was a former cop. Mean too and knows how to use force. I was a high school and college state wrestling champion for three years' running and could barely hold him off. Medium height, compact but built like a tank. Look at this," he said. Showing the guys his hands. He still had tremors.

"And that's after half a large coffee with cream and sugar. The guy's scary," he said.

"I hope she's worth it," Bruno said.

"I don't really know her. Nice looking trim brunette, around fifty I think. Other than hello once in the Super24 and 'assisting' her today, I've never really talked with her. I've seen her a time or two, like I said, and also coming and going once. She was in trouble and I helped her out. Bruno, I know you. You would've done the same," he said. Both of the guys nodded.

"What now then?" Ray said. Mike shrugged.

"All I know is the brunette was this psycho's ex-wife. I don't even know her name, but she thanked me for the help and told me I better watch my back. That I'm guaranteed on the guy's shit list now," he said. Ray shook his head.

"That's tough Mike. I hope you'll be ok. Guys like that, they don't forget," he said.

"Does he know your name?" Bruno said.

"I don't think so. Don't know how he could. He knows where his ex-wife lives and where she's staying. I told her my name's Mike. The police talked to her in the Super24 where she was waiting. He probably saw my truck. But it's a company truck. I don't know guys. I'm still glad I helped her out, though. But if he finds me, I'll have to deal with it then," he said.

"You got a heater in the truck?" Ray said.

"In the back. A rifle. It goes back in the house tonight."

Chapter 11

"Shit, that was close. They could've taken me in for questioning, if nothing else. Fortunately, they didn't know who I was." Rick Cameron was thinking what a break he just got. But lamented his untraceable gun was now gone.

"A small price to pay for getting out of there. If Mr. Goody Two Shoes hadn't come along, I'd be finished with my wife already," he said. He was at home trying to count his 'blessings.'

"Whitman's out of the picture, and now I'm high and dry. No way to get anymore inside information," he thought. Cameron was trying to console himself. He even considered just punting the whole matter. 'Quitting while he was ahead.' He shook his head and tried to think.

"Most days I'm off and I'll just have to use my time more wisely. Now, I've got to find that asshole who screwed everything up, too. I don't even know his name," he said. He fumed while walking around in his apartment. He had to work tonight and wouldn't be able to sleep now.

"Ok then. He was there in the morning. I'll look for him then. The truck said 'Kiewit' on the side. It's a construction company. He probably gets coffee there. And what was the misses doing going there, anyway? She didn't say anything to the guy when he opened the door, so she didn't know him."

"Now I've got to be careful. They surely know who I am with the images and plate number. Those kids—the cops who showed up didn't. Ok, it'll be old-fashioned gumshoe work," he said. With his 'plan,' formulated, Rick Cameron could get some fitful sleep for a while.

Mike removed the rifle from his truck at the house. It was getting dark by the time he got there and he carried the rifle in the case along with his wool blankets he'd usually take if he went hunting. In the garage, he had a locking supply closet. It wouldn't be hard for someone to break into, but it had mostly work tools inside. He placed the rifle behind all the stuff near the door and locked it.

"That's done. Now a cold brew and a sandwich," he said.

When Cameron's ex-wife got back to her sister's house, she welcomed the presence of the unmarked county cruiser.

"Of course, they'll call off the 'protection' the day before Cameron comes and kills us. Just like in the movies," she thought. She parked her car and walked over, tapping on the window. The officer inside saw her coming, but didn't expect her to tap on the window.

"Hello Ma'am," he said. Rolling down the window.

"Officer, thank you for what you're trying to do. If you don't know it already, my ex-husband followed me out of the neighborhood today when I left earlier. I'm too tired to get into the whole story. Call your Sergeant if you're interested. So you know, a good citizen stopped him from hurting—or killing me. He'll be worse now—even more dangerous. Just an FYI," she said.

"Yes Ma'am. They called me and told me. I'm glad you're ok," he said.

"Yeah. Hey, would you like a coffee or a soda? My sister has a coffeemaker, and I can get something for you."

"I'd love one. I'll even come to the—"

"I'll bring it out to you. My sister's not exactly thrilled with your department. It's not your fault, but I hope you understand. Just wait here, ok?" she said.

"No problem. I'll be leaving at noon when the replacement comes," he said. She paused and turned towards him.

"How long will the department be doing this? I mean, you can't do it forever, right?" she said.

"No, that's right. But a few days. Maybe even a week or ten days. We 'owe' you; and it's the least we can do," he said. What he didn't say was they were working on trying to come up with a sound arrest rationale to get Cameron off the streets. He didn't know all the details but was also not able to tell anyone; outside or inside the force. But they hoped Cameron would be apprehended on something and then they'd call off the 'protection' units. She nodded and headed to the house; and returned a few minutes later with a coffee.

"Thanks again. It can't be that great sitting here all day in the car," she said. The officer smiled and looked at her.

"We're glad to do it. Thank you for the coffee," he said. She nodded and walked back to the house. The officer took a welcome drink of the fresh brew. His brother was a cop up in Jersey City. He'd told him stories about how officers up there would occasionally cap guys like Cameron themselves. Then submit the 'appropriate' paperwork to their sergeant and wrap up the case. He wondered if it was true. He shrugged.

"Sounds good though," he thought.

At Henrico County Police, Sharon Wilder and two of her investigators worked hard, trying to piece together events from the past regarding former officer Richard Cameron. It was remarkable how crafty his reporting was. Like he was protecting himself from the future. Sharon Wilder was a worthy opponent, though. As good or better than any criminal mind could ever be. She had an idea she thought would do it. She beeped her secretary on the intercom, who came to the door.

"Jen, I need you to get me the files on the Gaston shooting Royland Whitman was involved in; along with the earliest arrest records Rick Cameron made when he was first on the force," she said.

"Is that it, Ms. Wilder?" she said.

"That's it for now. Except make sure you get the file with all the original materials, including the photographs taken at the Gaston shooting. Not just the summary file. I want that too, but everything we have on it," she said.

"Yes Ma'am. I'll get those files right now."

Mike wasn't in the habit of going to the west Henrico Super24 for coffees every day. It was a fluke the first day he'd gone there and met the former Mrs. Cameron. Because he'd met her, more out of curiosity than anything else, he'd stop there from time to time. Usually stopping at 7-Eleven or the Super24 up near the highway where the crew was working. Now, though, he'd cooled to the idea of going there; for a while anyway. He doubted 'Georgia' would go there much, either. Her ex was a genuine piece of work. But it'd been a few days, and without thinking, one day he pulled in for coffees. It wasn't far from his house and he could head straight to the site from there. He got the usual three large cups with all the fixin's and went back to the truck. His phone rang right as he was about to start up and drive out.

"This is Mike."

"Mike, it's Milt. I've got some good news for you. You can pass it on to the rest of the guys, too. The Virginia highway department's granted the next two segments of toll road to Kiewit. I've assigned all three of you," he said.

"Milt, that's fabulous. We'll all be able to stay here in Virginia then. Between what we have left now and those runs, that's probably over eighteen months of work. Maybe more," he said.

"Right. It's official—inked. I'm ecstatic and knew you'd be happy to hear the news," Cross said. Mike was buckling his seatbelt and about to start the truck, and saw a dark gray Jeep Wrangler pull into the Super24, which drove towards the gas pumps. It was one of many vehicles he'd seen coming and going. He kind of liked Wranglers. At least what they looked like. He never thought they were practical for his purposes—not enough room for a full hunting kit or to tie down a deer in the back. He started the engine while listening to Milt, then saw the driver. The window was down, and it was you-know-who, in the flesh. The Jeep pulled up to the farthest away pump, positioned so from where Mike sat he couldn't see the passenger. Mike waited a moment, hoping he'd see him get out to pump gas. When he realized that wasn't happening, he started driving out. He looked through the passenger side window as he did and saw him standing just outside his Jeep, watching Mike. Nonchalant. The message was clear; 'I see you. I haven't forgotten.'

"Asshole," Mike said, talking to himself. He took a deep breath and realized he was shaking.

"Ok, thank you for your time. If we have anything else we need, we'll call you," the officer said.

"No problem at all. Glad to answer your questions," he said. It was Dave Manfield, regional manager of Seven Gates Private Security. The company Rick Cameron worked for as a security guard. An investigator from Henrico County Police stopped by to ask some questions about Cameron's employment there. And what kind of work record he had?

"Reliable but rough around the edges," Manfield said. What he didn't say was the guy made him nervous. It's true, he was willing to take the more dangerous job assignments, and that was helpful. But something about the guy made him wary. After the officer left, he relayed to the company owner details of the police visit. He'd already told him they were coming and was supposed to call once they left.

"Dave, did he say why they were asking about him?" It was the owner, Zach Meyer.

"Not really Zach. He said it was basically routine, about a matter they needed some clarification on. That he may have been a witness to an incident several years ago, and they were concerned it may have affected him somehow. He didn't say exactly what he wanted, though."

"Yeah, ok. The thing is, the police rarely come around if they're not looking for something. Could be nothing, but let me know immediately if they call or come back," he said.

"Yes Sir. I will," he said. When they'd hung up, Zach Meyer looked over the notes he'd taken.

"It doesn't make sense. The guy is in the public records. The police could've stopped at his apartment themselves. It doesn't add up," he thought. He jotted down a couple additional things he thought of, checked everything over, then made a call to a friend of his. Meyer was no stranger to law enforcement; having gotten into the business because of what'd he'd learned from some people he knew in law enforcement who suggested private security was a good business idea. He picked up the phone and called a friend at the FBI. He held the receiver near his ear, waiting. Fourth ring, fifth coming up.

"Smithfield," the voice said. A moment before, Meyer was about to hang up.

"Gordie, it's Zach," he said. Gordie was Gordon Smithfield's nick name.

"Zach, long time no hear. Good to hear your voice, my friend. How's business?" he said.

"Pretty good. Not always easy, but holding our own and growing. Slow but sure," he said.

"Good. Glad to hear it. What can I do for you?" he said.

"I need a favor, Gordie." Silence. After a pregnant pause, Smithfield chuckled.

"Zach, I'll call you right back. Sit tight, ok?" he said. The receiver clicked off. Zach waited. Nearly two full minutes later, his cell rang.

"I'm here," Zach said.

"What's the name and what do you need? I do this only because I know you wouldn't ask if you didn't think it was a problem," he said.

"I know. I think it is. Name is Richard Cameron. An employee we hired a few years ago. Edgy guy. Former police officer from Henrico County Police Department. Said he left the force on good terms. I did the usual record check that I have access to. Clean. Hired him and he's reliable, but I always have to remind myself I wouldn't want to be on his wrong side. He makes my manager Dave Manfield nervous too. No particular issue here, but today a Henrico County Police investigator visited my manager asking about him. He said 'it's mainly routine.' I know it never is. That's the short version," he said.

"Got it. If he's a bad person and I find out, I can't help you with the fallout. You understand, right?" Smithfield said.

"I know. Let me know what you can, then we'll talk about it," he said.

"I'll see what I can find and get back to you tomorrow," he said.

"Gordie. Thanks, I appreciate it," he said.

"Always glad to help a friend. Talk to you tomorrow," he said. The phone clicked off and Meyer set the phone down on his desk. He thought about when he'd hired him.

"Most men don't walk from a six figure, or close to it, police officer position," he said. He'd thought of it, but everything was clean. And it's not always true—some men do leave. But they have a better story than Rick Cameron did. Meyer tucked the notes into a file and hoped for the best.

Chapter 12

"I'll have to move again. And I don't want to deal with it anymore, Phoebe. I'm so tired of this and wish I listened to Dad all those years ago. I know it's pointless now to say what I should've, could've, or would've done. But there you have it," she said. Phoebe and her sister sat and talked at the house. Phoebe knew her sister was considering leaving and going back to her own house in Atlanta. She figured she couldn't get him off the streets and being further away would make it more trouble for him to get to her. Not impossible, but more difficult. Phoebe sat silently, trying to think of something she could say. She still thought it would be better for her sister to stay with her. At least for a little while longer. Rather than say anything, she got up and made some tea. She set their cups down and stood by the edge of the table.

"Don't go. Not yet. Please," she said. Her sister's eyes glassed over with wetness. She shook her head, wiped her eyes, and smiled.

"Sit down Phoebe. I'll stay. For a couple more days, anyway. I love it up here in Virginia. I never wanted to leave. How about I take the two of us to dinner tonight?" she said.

"I'd like that," were the last words she got out before she broke down and sobbed. Her sister got up and put her arms around her shoulders and stood there. They were both glad to know they'd be together at least a little longer.

"None of this is on public record, Zach. I had to call in a big favor to get this. If you tell anyone these details I'll still love you but there won't be any more favors, ok?" It was Gordon Smithfield who'd called Zach Meyer.

"I appreciate you giving me the warning. I wouldn't betray your trust for anything, Gordie," he said.

"I know. But this was tough to get, and I had to say it. Now listen, Rick Cameron was termed for police brutality. It was a sealed action. Which is unusual, as IAD usually prosecutes. To me what's worse though, and this is the part that's essential you keep to yourself, his ex-wife divorced him better than a year prior to the termination in a quiet private divorce. The only reason I found this out was the Dad had pictures of his daughter's 'injuries' which he'd submitted to his own police department. Someone I know saw them. I don't want to say anything else, but if it was my daughter, I would've 'disappeared' the guy myself. And I mean it," he said. Meyer let out a low whistle.

"Ok Gordie, so what do you recommend? Leave things be, and let the guy fall on his own sword?" he said. Gordie was quiet and Zach waited.

"Zach, I don't know. Someone was protecting or protected him. And if you ask me, someone's after him now. I can't find out any more than I already did. What would I do? If you let him go, term him that is, it could trip him over the edge. With this type, anything's possible. You follow me?" he said.

"Loud and clear, my friend. My gut reaction is find a way to get rid of him. Just knowing this puts me on edge. But I've weathered some difficult situations so I can probably do it," he said.

"Zach, cooperate with the police, but maybe you should let it ride for now. You didn't know this right? It's not public information. He's been ok up to now. Unless he gives you a good reason, consider leaving well enough alone; for now, anyway. And remember, don't do anything different from what you've been doing. He'll know you know something if it's not standard operating procedure for the business. These guys can be ok, in fact very reliable, if no one rocks their boat," he said.

"Right. I get it. He didn't do anything to me either. And we had trouble getting anyone to take the warehouse job he's assigned to. Scary area but doesn't faze him at all. It's like he's walking around at a park," he said.

"The problem with many, if not most of these guys, is their troubles stay with them. They stabilize for a while, then when something goes wrong, they need to find someone to take it out on. But it can take a long time for that to happen. And it probably wouldn't be you; as long as you observe company protocol," he said.

"I owe you Gordie. This doesn't go anywhere, but I'm glad to know it. Thank you again," he said.

"Zach, if something happens—like the guy's behavior changes suddenly—call me ok?"

"I will. Thanks again Gordie."

Rick Cameron reported to his warehouse shift on time, early in fact. What he usually did. As much as he missed the badge, the police system, and mostly the power of the state, he knew they could 'turn on you.' That was his perspective on what happened to him. He thought being an enforcer for Stalin or Mao; that would be real power.

"But if they 'turn on you' there, your goose really would be cooked. Shot the same day," he thought.

"You can't win either way," he mused. Making a visual today on the guy that hurt him and caused him to lose his gun the other day was a break. He'd been going there almost every work day about the time he'd run into him with his ex. Using a 'poor man's' stake out. He would park his Wrangler in a warehouse parking lot not far away and walk over. Get a coffee and make himself invisible. Mainly watching. He thought he might even be able to spot the bitch, too—his ex. She never showed.

"The guy first," he said. Starting his first walk around the warehouse for the evening. He took a sip of his fresh black coffee as he made his way around.

"Life is good," he thought.

Netherland never got her name.

"I said 'Georgia.' Didn't know what else to say," he thought. Mike wanted to say 'hello' before she left. It was a bad morning—for both of them. Now it'd been a few of days since he'd seen her ex-husband standing watching him from the gas pump at the Super24. He hated the idea someone was out there looking for him.

"It's got to be hell for her. 'Cameron,' he heard the police say; could be a first or last name. Probably the last name," he thought.

"Ok, today it's coffees at 7-Eleven. I don't have the time or inclination for a fight right now," he thought. He got three large Brazilian dark roasts with a small bag of creams and sugars. He mixed his up in the store. When he walked out, he stopped a moment and looked around. He shook his head and walked straight to his truck.

"Now I know how Andy Warhol must've felt all those years; after that psycho Valerie Solanas shot him full of holes and almost killed him. Warhol was never the same after that, barely surviving the shooting, and they let her go with a slap on the wrist. Vowing, she'd eventually kill him when she got another chance. Poor Warhol had to live the whole rest of his life with Solanas out there. She died two months after he did. He was looking over his shoulder for the entire rest of his life after that. Terrible way to live," he thought. Mike racked his brains out, trying to remember who said a quote he was thinking about.

"Joseph Heller. That's who it is," he remembered.

"Just because you're paranoid doesn't mean someone's not after you." From what she'd told him that day, though, it's a lot worse for her. Mike had to keep reminding himself what his own father'd told him all those years ago. He knew his old dad was right; hard as it was to live it.

"This assignment's ending? The warehouse I'm assigned to?" he said. It was Rick Cameron talking to his manager, Dave Manfield.

"Yep. We got word today. It's possible it'll revive later. Otherwise, after two weeks, we're assigning you to a day route. Frankly, it's less of a headache and you'll be able to get back to sleeping in at night. It's forty minutes south of here, near Chesterfield Airport. Ten, maybe fifteen minutes further than you go now. Easy trip—against traffic too," he said.

"Is there anyone else I can switch with on another night assignment?" he said.

"Rick, we don't have a lot of night assignments. I didn't realize you preferred the late shifts, and we've already designated you for the new assignment. Your night assignment was a fluke, and no one else wanted it. We're surprised you didn't request a day assignment yourself already. You've been a good soldier, and it's also helped you get to a higher pay rate too," he said.

"No, I appreciate it, Dave. It's just I've gotten used to this schedule. It's all right. That's the way it is, but if anything changes or anyone wants to switch with me—from another night assignment—let me know, ok?" he said.

"Yeah, I will Rick. You've still got two weeks, though, so that's not bad. You can start getting yourself adjusted to day work again," he said. Dave was trying to be encouraging. He was a decent, friendly guy and thought Cameron'd be happier. He'd been in the business a while and only a few guys ever preferred nights. It was lonely and usually carried greater risk. Neighborhoods closer to industrial parks weren't always the best.

"Yeah. Ok thanks Dave," he said. Rick Cameron'd been called to the office so Manfield could tell him about the upcoming schedule change. He watched out the office window as Cameron walked back out to his Wrangler and shook his head.

"Everyone's different. Guess he just likes the night work," he said. He shrugged, then called Zach Meyer to tell him how Cameron took the assignment change. Meyer rarely cared about these kinds of matters unless there was a problem. He'd told him to call him after he'd talked with Rick. Dave thought maybe it was because the police had been by recently to ask some questions about the guy.

"Did he get angry at all?" Zach said.

"No, not really. He definitely didn't expect a change. He asked if he could stay on nights by switching with someone else. I told him we'd already assigned him and didn't commit to getting into that idea. He was ok. It seemed more to me like he considered a day shift an inconvenience. Like he had something else he was doing then. I can't imagine anyone could have two jobs like this, though," he said.

"Ok thanks Dave. It's probably nothing but the police coming by concerned me. He's done nothing to hurt us, but having a past in law enforcement, I know the police rarely come by for 'routine matters.' Anyway thanks," he said.

"No problem Zach. Of course, anything I can do for you, I'm here. I mean, you've given me a good career here and have been good to me. You name it, I'll do whatever you need," he said.

"Yeah, Dave, I'm glad to have you with me. With this guy, though, anything at all out of the ordinary—no matter how small it may seem to you—you gotta call me. You have my cell and I don't care what time it is, call me ok?"

"Yeah sure. You know I will, man," he said.

"If he's irked, there's no creamer for the coffee, then don't call me. Work related or behavior issues is what I mean," he said.

"Yep, I understand," Dave said. When they'd hung up, Meyer added some notes to his file. He was trying to not pay attention to the issues Gordie dug up about the guy. Cameron hadn't hurt them and, unlike a police department, he had a lesser issue with public perception. But the business was growing now and getting an excellent reputation. Any kind of blot could stall the growth he'd finally been achieving. He thought it was a blessing to lose the gig with the warehouse by the industrial park. It would've been a way to let him go. A 'hey Cameron, we're sorry. We had no idea they wouldn't need us anymore,' story. Pay him two weeks' severance plus the two last weeks. Then call it a day. He's gone and everyone's happy.

"At least I'd be happy," he thought. But he hadn't told Dave not to reassign him if something else came up.

"Too late now," he said. He put the papers and notes back in the file and stood up.

"I've got to get a drink."

Chapter 13

Behind the wooded area, south of the Super24, was an industrial parking area shared by two businesses. One, a large auto mart that leases space to park vehicle overages along with an auction lot for cars they want to dump, and sell to smaller or individual car dealers. The auto mart also has some attendants who move cars around, bring cars over, and also assist with their periodic car auctions. Local towing and small industrial truck businesses that need a place to exchange loads, check truck routes and load assignments before and after their trips use the other part of the lot.

Marty Goldman had been working for Eastern Motors for over a year. He liked cars and though the pay was only minimum wage when he started, the owner—who he couldn't tell if he was Russian, Greek, or Arabian—liked him. Marty hustled and paid attention to details. He also made himself available for coffee runs, picking up clothes from the cleaners; or any other odd jobs he'd do without complaint. Frankly, he liked the guys and was glad to be working outside most of the time. A win-win for everyone. They'd recently upped his pay to twenty-two bucks an hour and from time to time, they would even slip him an extra twenty. Sometimes a couple. Just because "we like you, kid," they'd say. He knew there was probably more money to be made selling cars, but he wasn't interested.

"Too much pressure," he thought. He liked the simplicity of what he was doing just fine. He lived with his older brother, who let him use the spare bedroom and didn't charge him for staying. One thing Marty had was a good eye and great attention to detail. Day in and day out, he'd be back and forth to the back lots: ten, twenty—sometime even thirty times or more. In the evening when he walked back there, he could tell if a bulb was out in the perimeter overhead lights just by the change in the way light and shadows were cast. There was video surveillance, but only accessed it after there was a problem. They could look back on a sequence of still images and see what happened if a car was damaged or stolen. Not a common occurrence. Marty's eyes were still better. And the week after Dave Manfield told Rick Cameron about his upcoming schedule change, Marty noticed something. A dark gray two door Jeep Wrangler soft top parked in the non auction lot. That type of thing rarely bothered him here and there. It's just it was in a different spot each day he saw it and it was every day for the last four days. The fourth time he saw it, he did what he always did, wrote the plate number down and took a picture of the vehicle from a couple of different angles on his iPhone.

"Here Patty. Find out who's this is. It's been parking in the employee and truck overflow lot every day for the last four or five days. Probably nothing but just good to know. The usual," he said.

"Sure. Ever see who it is?" she said. Marty shook his head.

"I haven't seen anyone get in or out. It only made me curious because it's always in a different spot. Same area, but whoever's parking there is trying to make it blend into a group of other vehicles. Wranglers stand out though," he said.

"I'll call my buddy at DMV and get a name," she said.

"Thanks P." She looked up at him and shook her head.

"What?" he said.

"P? What's P?" she said.

"I thought it'd be cool. P. You don't like it?" She shrugged, then smiled.

"It's ok. M," she said. Marty laughed and walked away.

No one on a stakeout can make someone show up. But if you're consistent and patient, it can be effective. Cameron'd been every day from six in the morning to noon. He'd get a coffee and 'chill' in the woods. Walk around and make like he was on a work break.

"It's getting tiresome," he thought. It was Friday. He had a little more than a week left before his new shift change at work.

"He'll be back," he said. Never a certainty, of course, but if you know that's where the fish usually are, stay there and wait. The idea of going to Phoebe's house was a bust. Especially after the incident with the gun and the police watch.

"I'd be picked up for sure. Definitely not worth the risk over there," he thought. Cameron wished he could just sit in his vehicle and watch all day in the lot. He didn't like the risk of being spotted by Henrico's finest though. Shortly after noon, he grabbed another coffee and walked back to his Jeep through the woods.

"Hey are you Richard Cameron?" a voice said. He turned and saw a young guy talking to him. Pleasant. But that he knew his name startled him. Cameron looked at the kid, then at his Wrangler. He softened a little.

"Yeah, that's me," he said. He realized it was probably protocol to get names of owners of unknown vehicles.

"The lot's so full at the Super24 I usually park back here. I come over on lunch break," he said.

"I understand. I'm Marty, I work at Eastern Motors across the way. You're not really supposed to park here. People do it but we have so many cars coming and going this week, we usually need most of the spots," he said.

"Sure, no problem, kid. I understand. I'll do something different next time," he said.

"I'm not trying to give you a hard time, Mr. Cameron. I'm a car mover and manage the vehicles back here. Just wanted to let you know," he said.

"Sure. I understand. It's ok. I would've done the same if I were in your shoes. I'm leaving now anyway, but thanks for telling me," he said.

"No problem. Must be a long lunch break; I've seen your Jeep here most all mornings. Wish I had that kind of breather," he said. Cameron nodded. Agitated, someone recognized he'd been there so long each day.

"You've got a good eye for details, Marty. See you around," he said. Cameron drove out and onto the road next to the lot and eyed the enormous parking lot there. But decided parking there the next day was too far away. It was too far, anyway. If he had to get out of dodge fast, it wouldn't work out so well.

"Just as well the kid spotted me," he thought. It ticked him off, though they looked up his name. He was glad he played it cool. Nice and friendly. He drove up to the Super24 lot and decided next time he'd park there, on the other side or maybe in the back corner on the front side and move all the way back.

"Yeah, that'll work. Now time to get a few hours of sleep," he thought. He drove home to get ready for tonight's shift in a few hours.

"I'll be back soon, Phoebe," she said. Phoebe stood, broken-hearted for her sister, and wishing she'd stay.

"I can't stay forever, you know. I've been up here now for six weeks. You could come down with me. Take some time off and drive to Atlanta. But I need to get back. I wish I never moved away in the first place, especially now that Cam has all the addresses," she said.

"I know. But you know, maybe I will come down. You're not going to change your mind. But I'm not going to stop trying to change it for you either," she said. Smiling. She'd already explained to the police she was going back to Atlanta, where she lived.

"All right, I'll take some time off and come down. I should get a gun first in case the asshole comes to Atlanta," she said. Her sister smiled. She wished it was that easy.

"It's not whether you have a gun but who has the drop," she thought. Cam told her that himself; way back when. They hugged goodbye, and she headed out of the drive. She only planned on coming up for two weeks at first, but stayed because of recent events. Her car was obviously packed for a trip; with a suitcase and piles of items in the back seat. In the trunk, she had her other travel bags.

"I can't be a hostage up here forever, you know," she said.

"Ms. Cameron, are you sure you're not willing to stay a little longer? Even a few more days?" the officer said.

"What's going to be different in a few days?" she said. The officer didn't know for sure, but Sergeant Jamison said Wilder was poised for something. She'd told him and the Captain to 'be ready soon.' It was Saturday morning and Cameron's ex thought it was as good a morning to go home as any.

"Everything else happened on a weekday," she said.

The Super24 was very busy for a Saturday morning. Mike, like almost every Saturday, was on his way to the job site for a 'short' work day. He expected it to be a long one today, though, despite their best efforts. Rain was coming Monday, and they had work that had to be completed while the conditions were dry. Mike, Ray, Bruno, and almost a half regular crew. Not to mention some heavy Caterpillar equipment, including a large crane they were leasing for two weeks with its operator. A big workday for a Saturday. When Mike pulled in to get some coffees and breakfast sandwiches, he had to wait to get a spot to back into. When he got out of the cab, he walked to the back truck bed to make sure he had the plans and the material integrity test equipment he'd need for checking concrete hardness on pillars they poured a two days ago. His back was to the woods behind him while he moved things around.

"Here they are. And everything else we need too," he said. He stepped backward to get out of the bed and onto the ground, and reached to close the gate. He was jerked back as he leaned to lift it up. Grabbed from behind with huge force. He instinctively braced himself to prevent whoever it was from getting a secure hold. Mike already knew who it had to be and did his best to brace himself and prepare for a struggle. The guy was strong—and mean. A bad combination. Mike tried to swing his legs back underneath to clip the guy's feet. Even with the smallest loss of balance, he could bring the guy to the ground; where Mike could do his best work. Cameron was ready though and kept his lower legs further back. He cinched up on Netherland's arm and right shoulder, with no regard whether he broke or tore any bones or ligaments. It's what he wanted. Netherland was taller and built bigger, but Cameron was no stranger to using force and knew how to use it well. He had Netherland in a nearly intractable grip, holding him around his upper torso so he couldn't get his left arm anywhere near him. Cameron knew if the guy got a chance, his 'free' arm would be a big problem.

"Now I'm gonna hurt you bad," Cameron said. He pulled him backwards; they were mainly out of view because they were behind the back of the truck. Cameron knew if anyone came to their car near where he was, they'd see them struggling. Cameron made as if he would pull the two of them into the woods. Mike knew enough about hunting that he would not let that happen. He was six inches taller than Rick Cameron and, using his body as a lever, he set up a sway. Slight at first; intending to use the weight of his upper body to pull forward. That's when he felt a sharp jab pierce his side. He winced and maintained his plan. He could tell it was a deep wound but missed the kidney.

"Ok, here we go," Mike thought.

"Don't try it again," Cameron said. He was close to Netherland's ear and Mike knew the guy was struggling for all he was worth to hold him. Cameron pulled his right arm lower and harder. An effort to inflict more pain and damage. Mike winced but forced himself on. He knew he'd torn his rotator cuff and also pulled the ball out of the socket. Things he learned long ago as a competitive wrestler.

"Hurts, doesn't it asshole? Relax and it'll be over soon," Cameron said. He made a forceful movement to pull Netherland back and made a good go of it. But stumbled a little on a root. That was the break Mike needed.

"Forget the knife Mike; go!" he thought. It was now or never to force him off balance. Mike pulled from the top, using everything he had, deciding to 'ignore' the pain. Cameron didn't realize just how big or capable Mike was. The pain was excruciating, but he used every sinew he could get command of and forward and down they went. Mike retracted his own head and shoulder to avoid the rear truck gate that was still down. In so doing, they not only went down in the forward direction, but Rick Cameron's head solidly smashed into the tailgate edge. A full on slam, in fact, splitting the skin of his forehead down to the bone. Cameron no longer had any grip to speak of on Mike, who pulled himself free, turning around to face Rick Cameron. Unbeknownst to either of them, Rick Cameron's ex-wife had pulled into the Super24 not long before and saw Mike's Kiewit truck. Deciding she'd say goodbye, she started over and saw from around the corner the two men near the edge of the woods. She ran into the store and straight to the manager's office.

"Call the police. There are two men fighting and bleeding near the edge of the woods. One's Richard Cameron, my ex-husband. Do it now, do you hear me? He's armed and dangerous," she said. Several people started running and an assistant manager went into the manager's office and pressed the speed dial 911 button.

She put her left hand over her mouth and went back outside, staying as close as she could to the front of the store. She saw Mike looking towards the woods, standing on the grass by the curb. His right arm was hanging funny and blood was pouring out of his left side, just above his kidney. His pants and shirt soaked with blood. Rick Cameron stood up, looking at Mike. Bleeding badly from the vicious rap on his head to the rear gate of Mike's Silverado. Both men were panting heavily. Mike saw Cameron could take pain, too. But he had a lot of blood getting in his face and eyes. Frozen in space and time, the two men looked at each other, waiting. "The first one who moves loses," is what Coach McGuire always told the wrestlers. Each man readying themselves. Not for a medal, but for their life.

Chapter 14

"All right, we got him. Bring this to the Captain. I'll be right over. Show him the cover sheet—that's all he'll be interested in, anyway. I'll bring the full file over in five minutes. Tell him to wait until I get there," she said. Sharon Wilder and Gabe Whelan had their case. The Whitman shooting and one other act of police brutality they'd overlooked which resulted in a brain damaged arrestee. Whelan knocked on the Captain's door, who'd already been standing by.

"Captain, it's Gabe Whelan. Sharon sent me over with the summary of the file. The top sheet inside will have everything you'll probably want to see," he said.

"Come in Whelan. Have a seat," he said. Gabe Whelan plopped the file politely on the captain's desk and sat down. Mattias opened the cover and looked it over carefully, nodding. He turned and looked at Whelan.

"I take it Sharon's coming in a minute?' he said.

"She's on her way. She wants to review a few items when she gets here," he said. Mattias smiled and looked at the overview sheet again.

"He's not getting a pass this time. That's for damn sure, Whelan," he said. Sharon Wilder walked in right as he closed

102

the file folder. She closed the captain's door and sat down in the chair beside Whelan.

"Hello Sharon. Whelan just gave me the sum of it and said you were coming."

"Everything you see there is more than enough for an arrest and conviction. We also have the unregistered modified .38 special caliber revolver with the replacement smooth bore barrel. Not necessarily illegal, but we all know why that barrel was put on the gun. If that's not enough, the gun has no serial number. Welded over and ground. The frame, grip and even the micro number under the screw plate. Not by itself illegal. But it won't help a court case. And that's where this is going. That's the last part of the story I wanted you to know. Captain, do you have any questions for me?" she said.

"No," he said.

"I'll wait right here until the arrest and APB are issued," she said. Mattias beeped a number on his intercom. There was a sequence of buzz sounds. A click, then a voice.

"Jamison here."

"Sergeant it's the Captain. I'm in my office with Sharon Wilder and Officer Gabe Whelan. Put out an immediate arrest APB for Richard Cameron. Effective as soon as you can get it in order. I'm here in my office for any signatures," he said.

"Consider it done. You know it'll probably be tomorrow before—"

"Just get it out there. I understand it probably won't be on the police wire until early in the morning," he said.

"Yes Sir," he said. They clicked off. It was Friday afternoon just after three.

"Hurts doesn't it?" Mike said. He saw the knife in Cameron's hand. A curved blade Japanese 'fighting' knife. He wondered how he could stab him the way he was holding him. What Cameron didn't count on was Mike's tenacity; who'd spent enough time on the matts in training and competitions to know holding fast when there's not much left in you is usually the difference between winning and losing.

"After I finish you, I'll get my wife," Cameron said. He made a fast wipe of his face, trying to get some of the blood off; which was dripping profusely down from his head. Mike didn't say a word. He stood waiting and watching. Cameron was dazed, but dangerous. Like a gambler doubling down on a loss; Mike knew he'd get reckless.

Three cruisers were en route. Flashers full on, no sirens. They couldn't be driving any faster without a pilot's license.

"Don't let him get away. Pretend it's your wife he's trying to kill," were Jamison's last words.

The two men moved slowly, both waiting for someone to make the first move.

"The one on higher ground wins; every time. Dead or alive," his father'd said. Mike was calm, knowing it would be over soon. Hurt and weak, he kept his eyes on point. Cameron heard the cars. He knew the sound of a multi-car arrival. He swiped with the knife at Mike. A one–two, back and forth swing. He hoped to cut Netherland, get rid of him as a threat so he could run.

"Missed. He can move," he thought. Feverish to get away, he looked for any break. He knew if they went to the ground, he'd be finished. Cameron's eyes darted this way and that. He tried again with the knife and missed. Cruisers were pulling into the Super24 so fast you could hear the asphalt crackling. Mike made the slightest turn to see what it was. And when he looked back, Cameron was gone. He could hear him running through the woods, but stood where he was and put his hands on his knees. The pain in his right shoulder was so bad that he jerked involuntarily. He reached around with his left arm and could feel he was sodden with blood on his back left side. He pressed the area and winced, but thought the blood flow had slowed.

"Whew, the guy's fast," Mike said. He leaned heavily against his truck, his energy waning now, and saw two police officers running into the woods with guns drawn. A fourth police vehicle pulled in—a large SUV. Three officers got out, one coming over to Mike.

"Sir, we have a Henrico County EMT vehicle on the way. And I'm a medic trained officer. Mind if I look at that wound?" he said. Mike moved his hand away so he could check it.

"He missed the kidney," Mike said. The officer looked up, then back at the wound.

"You're a hunter?" the officer said. Mike nodded.

"What's your name?' he said.

"Mike. Mike Netherland," he said.

"Hold tight Mr. Netherland. I'm going to wipe this wound off and tape a gauze over it until EMT gets here," he said. Mike nodded again. Too pooped to even use his vocal cords. The two officers in the woods were some of the best footmen in Jamison's squad. They triangulated based on where they heard footsteps, keeping each other in sight. Jamison briefed them and explained that Cameron knew what he was doing. He'd be dangerous and hard to catch if he was on the run. In the woods, the officers stood waiting and didn't hear anything. They kept their guns at the ready, barrels towards the ground but easy to bring to bear when needed.

Willie Burnham had passed through Central Virginia many times. He rarely stopped in Virginia, though. The last time he actually made a stop in the region was in Petersburg, and that was a few years back. Today he picked up a 'heavy.' What truckers refer to as a full capacity load. Industrial concrete forms, each packed in their own box and stacked evenly in the large trailer he was pulling. He'd taken a wrong exit and was running behind, now just outside the western side of Richmond City on Broad Street. Unfamiliar with the town, he parked the truck to look around. He needed to eat anyway and thought he'd get a coffee to take with him on the road. The truck he drove was a brand new Peterbilt low pressure turbo diesel. Their heaviest duty model with a sleeper cab. A state-of-the-art vehicle his company, Western Shipping, had recently purchased to replace several of their worn out trucks. Burnham was one of their best and most reliable drivers, based out of Dallas, Texas. He saw signs that said 'Willow Lawn.' He'd gotten something to eat at a Panera Bread then went back to the truck with his coffee. His phone ring and he picked up. He already knew it would be dispatch.

"Hello. This is Willie," he said.

"Hey Willie. Are you on the road yet?" It was Chip, the dispatch manager.

"Just about Chip. Getting on right now. I got lost after I picked up the load and needed lunch anyway," he said.

"Ok good. You're not late, but there's a $500 cash bonus for you if you can get the load delivered tomorrow by six p.m. There's not much fat in the schedule, but it's a straightforward drive once you're on the highway. You know I never press you to run too hard. So if you don't make it, it's not a problem. But if you do, it's $500 cash," he said.

"I'll get the $500 or I'm not Willie Burnham," he said. There was chuckling on the other end.

"I thought you'd say that. Look, don't rush. Understand? You're a good driver. It's a nice little chunk of change but drive safe," he said.

"Understood. I'll be careful. Let me get going and I'll see what I can do," he said. He hopped into the new Pete, started her up and after he'd looked at the truck advised route for a 'heavy,' from where he was, he was off down Broad Street, heading west.

"Should be no sweat," he said. Burnham put his iPhone on the mount and the route to destination looked like it'd be clear of traffic and bad weather the whole way. He took a pull of Panera coffee and tooled down the road.

"I'm even in sync with the lights—how about that?"

Cars were gingerly coming and going at the Super24, seeing multiple Henrico County Police cruisers with their flashers on. There was even one SUV with two officers that formed a car 'checkpoint' for vehicles leaving out of the westward store exit.

"It's only a matter of time," the officer in the woods thought. With only the two of them, they couldn't perform a full sweep of the wooded area, but it wasn't possible to make a request at the moment on the radio or they'd give up their position. Cars were starting and stopping their engines as they came and went, so it didn't cause any concern when the dark gray Jeep Wrangler started. It was a stock engine and muffler, so made no out of the ordinary noise. The two officers in the woods heard a vehicle take off aggressively and started running out.

"He won't get out," the one said. They ran out into the parking lot only to see the dark gray Wrangler driving dangerously fast in a parking lot. Rick Cameron sped out left to the still open passage to the road. He struck a workman, who suffered a badly broken arm and several bruised ribs. In the clearing, the two officers from the woods held their guns pointed towards the ground. There was no way they could take a shot, and he was driving away. The two officers stood together as the Wrangler sped out.

"We'll have him in five minutes," the one said. They holstered their guns and made haste to get to their cars.

"Cameron, stop. Don't do it," an officer hollered as he drove through the one car path out of the Super24. He signaled two other officers to head out and get him. They drove to the next exit, which would put them on Broad Street heading west, where Cameron would be. Two officers stood by as Cameron barely made it through the one car passageway. A fluke because no one was coming in the moment he sped out. The moment he was clear of the police cars, everyone there saw Cameron's left hand sticking high in the air out of the side of the Wrangler. His middle finger and arm were like a temple monument no one could miss. Driving with only one hand momentarily, flipping the bird like he did, he recklessly sped directly out into the road. Broad Street west, the ramp to I-64 dead ahead. The two Henrico County Police cruisers poised to make chase. And the two officers from the woods shaking their heads.

No one saw or heard the smooth, quiet Peterbilt turbo diesel. No one except Rick Cameron. It was the last thing he saw when Willie Burnham plowed into his sideways Jeep Wrangler at forty-nine miles an hour. It may as well have been two hundred miles an hour as far as Rick Cameron was concerned. Several people watching turned away. But not everyone. Willy Burnham couldn't do a thing to prevent the crash. Moving left or right would've killed a lot more people. He did what any well-trained tractor trailer driver did and slowed gradually, continuing in a straight line when there was no safe alternative. One of the strangest things one officer there had ever seen was the funny way Rick Cameron's left arm fell sideways with his middle finger still out. A short visual as he was pushed along in a straight line until Willie Burnham could bring the Pete to a complete stop.

In the ensuing fracas, it seemed like the entire Henrico County Police Force showed up. Cameron's ex saw everyone running to the road. Police officers were coming in and out and explained to the manager the main front entrance would be closed for several hours. Customers could use the rear entrance, but the store would probably have a lot fewer customers. Twenty minutes after Willie Burnham's Peterbilt plowed into the side of Rick Cameron's Jeep Wrangler, a high polish unmarked Henrico County vehicle pulled into the Super24 by the alternate entrance. It was Captain Mattias and Sergeant Jamison, paying a personal visit to the incident location.

"Looks like we'll be able to dispense with arrest and prosecution now," Jamison said. He was looking at the crushed dark gray Wrangler and the deceased Richard Cameron who'd need to be sawn out of the mangled Jeep. Blood leaked onto the ground below from the undercarriage floor drain. Jamison looked around inside, shook his head, and turned away.

"He's actually dead, right?" Phoebe Rinnder said. She'd forced her way through the police barrier to the wreckage, doing her best to peer inside the Wrangler that was crowded with police officers. Jamison turned to look at her; deciding to dispense with formalities and not bother asking who let the woman come through.

"Go ahead, look yourself," he said. He moved aside and waved a couple of officers aside so she could get closer. Phoebe took a good long look at her former brother-in-law. She never had the class her sister did, but as much as she wanted to spit on the ground, she refrained and looked at Jamison.

"Thanks for letting me see for myself," she said.

"Ma'am, he drove right into my path. There was nothing I could do," he said. It was Willie Burnham who thought the guy he hit might've been the woman's husband.

"Thank heavens," she said. And walked away.

Ten minutes earlier, Phoebe received a call from her sister, who told her there was a manhunt, then a crash out on Broad Street. Right in front of the Super24.

"I think Cam's been hit by a truck," she said.

"I'll be right over, sis," Phoebe said.

"There's no need to…" she started to say. But realized her sister'd already hung up. The icon on her phone showing the call had ended. She never even saw Phoebe come into the store parking lot. Mainly because the minute she arrived, she bolted from her car towards Broad Street where the mêlée was. When she left the crushed Wrangler, Phoebe walked back up to the store to see her sister.

"The son of a bitch is dead. And I mean dead like dead. They said he was killed almost instantly when the trucker hit him," Phoebe said.

"It's over now. For real Sis," she added. They were standing by her car, loaded to go back to Atlanta, and she fell onto Phoebe's shoulders. Phoebe held her. She wasn't crying. Broken, but still standing.

"Dad's going to want to know. You want me to call him?" Phoebe said.

"No. I'll call him. I'll do it right now," she said.

Chapter 15

Mike Netherland called Ray on the way to Henrico Doctor's Hospital while he was lying down in the EMT transport. He briefly explained he was in a bad tangle with Cameron.

"The guy's dead now," Mike said.

"You killed him?" Ray said.

"I would've if he tried to kill me again. He had me in a literal death grip; but I got free. He killed himself. But not before he tried to kill me first. Drove into the pathway of a Peterbilt headed to the highway ramp. T-boned with a full load," he said.

"Holy shit Mike," he said.

"Yeah, hey I'm a little weak right now. Can you call Milt? You'll have to run the site without me for a day or so. But you can always call me here. I'll be 'left handed' until they fix up my shoulder," he said.

"Yeah sure Mike. We'll be ok. I'll call him when I hang up with you. You'll be ok though, right?" Ray said.

"My right shoulder's in rough shape—real bad. He missed my kidney with his knife. Just barely. They tell me I'll live though," he said.

"Mr. Netherland you really should get off the phone," an EMT said in the vehicle said

"Ray, I'll call you as soon as I can. They're taking me to

Henrico Doctor's right now," he said.

"Mike, we'll come see you tonight. I'll call Cross right now," he said.

"Thanks Ray."

It took over four hours to clean up and clear the crash site on Broad Street. Lots of protocol, paperwork, and physical cleanup. A deceased body from a vehicle collision has to be removed near the scene, so that was a real time hit. The police spoke at length with Willie Burnham, who they let go after a couple of hours. Cleared completely as having any fault. He spoke with Chip and explained everything to him.

"Willie firstly are you ok—for real?" Chip said.

"Yeah, sure Chip. I was shook bad at first. But like I said, the guy drove right into my path. He wasn't looking out for traffic. There wasn't a damn thing I could do except start braking and continue straight. Just like they tell you in the 'book.' And the truck's fine. I know that's your next question. The reinforced front steel bumpers on these new Petes must be indestructible. A Couple of small dents and some paint scraped bad, otherwise pretty good. I'll send you a picture when we hang up. Nothing like the guy's Jeep I ran into. Anyway, the boys at the shop in Dallas'll be able to make it look like new," he said.

"Yeah good. Thanks Willie. Sorry you had to go through all that. I really am. You're more important than the truck, too. I hope you believe me. While I had you on the phone, I just thought I'd ask—"

"I know you love me, Chip. But it's an expensive truck. Bugs me too. The guy I hit—I hear he was a real bad character. A wife beater ex cop who tried to kill his former wife and a guy that helped her, too," he said. Chip was quiet for a moment.

"Well, at least the damage on the truck was for a 'good

cause.' I hate for anyone to get killed, but some people 'kill' themselves, you know?" he said.

"Yeah. I think this guy was one of `em," Willie said.

"Look Willie, I doubt you'll make the 6 p.m. tomorrow. I'm giving you the $500 myself; so take it easy. You get there when you get there. If they need anything else from you in Virginia, stay at a hotel. The company'll pick up the tab for you, my friend. Otherwise, see you when you get back to Dallas," he said.

Ray and Bruno both went to the hospital to see Mike after they wrapped up at the site for the day. Milt'd called him already and told him to rest and try to sit still. He wished him the best and asked if they should send an alternate highway engineer for a few days.

"You want to delay the project even more? Ray and Bruno have got it covered. I'm not brain damaged. At least no more than usual. They can call me or you for questions. Don't send anyone else unless I die on the operating table," Mike said. Milt laughed.

"Sounds like you're going to be ok Mike," he said.

"That highway's mine—I'll take care of it. I got two surgeries, back to back. I should be out of here in four days, tops. Maybe three. I won't be able to do anything with my right arm for a while. But they gave me permission to still use my brain," he said.

"I understand Mike. But make sure the guys know I'm here if you're not available and there's a problem, ok?" he said.

"Roger that. I don't want any screwups either, Milt," he said. Mike had a good but brief visit with the guys. His first shoulder surgery was in the morning and he was worn out and tired from all the events. Mostly, though, the damage to his shoulder just plain sucked the life out of him.

"Gentleman, Mr. Netherland has a big day tomorrow and

I'm going to have to ask you to leave. It's actually already past visiting hours," the nurse said.

"Ok Mike. We'll come by tomorrow. There's a lot going on at the site, Monday, but we know what to do. Get some rest," Bruno said.

"Thanks for coming guys. Call me anytime; I'll leave my phone on," he said. It didn't take long for them to get Mike set for the night. His vitals were good, but he was weak. He was out like a light and as much as he hated hospitals, the bed and some sleep were welcome. He wanted the surgeries over and done so he could just get out of the hospital and get back to work.

"Mr. Netherland, how're you feeling?" It was Doctor Reichert, the orthopedic surgeon who'd done the surgery already, along with a hospital nurse. They were checking in on him. Mike was half asleep, still but waking. And starving too. It was Sunday, late morning.

"Groggy, but I guess ok. How'd it go Doc?" he said.

"We did everything in a single surgery while we had you open. It's best that way if you can do it. That way, we don't have to take you apart and put you together twice. Especially the shoulder. It was a worse tear to your rotator cuff than we thought. Those are the tendons and muscles surrounding and connecting the bone to your shoulder underneath the clavicle. That was the hard part of the surgery—trying to reconnect those. And we were able to get the 'ball' of your humerus back in place while we were in there, too. We didn't think we'd be able to do everything in a single operation, but there you have it. The force the guy used on your arm was enough to do some serious damage, but amazingly, he didn't break any of your bones," Reichert said.

"We were in there a while. But I think that's going to do it. I hope you don't mind," he added.

"Doctor, as much as you can do in one procedure is fine with me," Mike said. He looked at his right arm, which was heavily bandaged and slung up tight. He tried to move it a little and winced.

"We have your arm immobilized as much as we can, so you can't to do that; move it around that is. The problem with the shoulder is you can't do much of anything without it. But for it to get better, you'll have to let it set for ten days with little to no movement. It's essential in order for it to heal properly," he said.

"Ten days without shaving or showering?" Mike said. Reichert smiled and nodded.

"Use an electric shaver with your left arm. The shower—without someone to help you, that's about right," he said.

"Ok, so when can I go home? And how about work—can I go to the site?" he said.

"You need to stay here until tomorrow, for sure. Maybe two days. I can't stop you, but strongly recommend you stay at home three or four days after you're released. It's just too easy to move your arm around and get a setback," he said. Mike nodded.

"I'll do what you say. I don't like the sitting still part but don't want to come back in here either," he said. Mike lay his head back, still tired. The nurse plumped up his pillow and adjusted him so he'd be comfortable.

"Thanks ma'am, I appreciate that," he said; always the gentleman.

"Ok Mr. Netherland. I'll check back in on you later this afternoon, near the end of the day. You get some rest and Charlotte, your nurse here. will take good care of you," he said.

"Thanks again Doc. I'm glad you don't have to go back in there again," he said. Reichert waved and headed out.

"Try to lay still, Mr. Netherland. And get some sleep too," Charlotte said. He nodded, closed his eyes and slept fitfully for a few hours. From in dreamland there was something making a noise. It went away and started again. A sharp knocking sound; three hard raps in a row. He woke and turned his head.

"Hello. Mind if we come in?" It was a woman's voice. Mike forced himself awake and looked towards the open door to his hospital room.

"Yeah, hey come on in," he said. Two women entered and stood near his bed. He looked at them and smiled.

"Georgia. And you're Phoebe, right?" he said. Phoebe turned to her sister with a puzzled expression on her face, then back to Mike.

"Hi Mike," 'Georgia' said. To Mike, she had the most beautiful smile a woman could have. Kind, gentle, and, most of all, relieved.

"Hey. Thanks for coming to see me. How are you two doing?" he said. Doing his best to sit up as much as possible in his bed. Not so easy with only one arm 'available.'

"Oh, don't do that Mike. It's ok, just stay laying down," Phoebe said.

"Georgia, are you ok?" he said. Phoebe turned and looked at her sister again with a 'what's up?' expression on her face. Her sister was smiling.

"Mike, he would've killed you," she said. She paused, then wiped her eye, which was glassing up.

"I'm glad he didn't," she added.

"And he won't be able to now, either. The bastard's dead," Phoebe said. Mike couldn't help laughing out loud, his body heaving up and down as he did. He couldn't decide if the pain was worth the trade for the laughter.

"Oh, be careful. See what you made him do," she said.

"It's good for him. It'll help him heal faster, too," Phoebe said. Her sister gave her the 'eye.' And bit her lower lip.

"Yeah, it's ok," he said. Still trying not to laugh.

"See, he's ok. By the way, my sister's name is—"

"Georgia. It's Georgia," she said. Phoebe shook her head and wondered what'd gotten into her sister. Truthfully, she didn't care now. So long as her sister didn't have to live with that psychopath out there anymore, she'd be happy to call her Tinker bell.

"You two are sisters?" he said. Half question, half statement. They nodded.

"Hey Georgia, how about a coffee when I get out of here? Maybe dinner or lunch with that too?" he said.

"Sure," she said.

"Sure? What do you mean 'sure?' That'd be a 'yes' Mike, in case you were wondering," Phoebe said, chiming in. His eyes fixed on Georgia.

"You have your phone?" 'Georgia' said, talking to Mike. With his right arm, he began reaching for it. He didn't need to remind himself it was a bad idea; his shoulder doing it for him. Using his left hand, he picked up the phone.

"You ready? My number is...," she said, reading off the digits. Phoebe raised her eyebrows. He typed along while she spoke. Mike pressed 'call' and her phone started, then he ended the call.

"There. You have my number now, too. I'm Mike Netherland. You probably already know that, don't you?" he said.

"I do. And Mike, the answer's yes. 'Sure' meant yes," she said. He looked at her, smiling. Nodding his head.

"Georgia, I'll call you. I'll be out of here in two days. Keep your calendar open for Sunday," he said.

"Wait a minute. You're going back this week. How're you —" Phoebe said.

"I'm staying. I forgot to tell you. And next week I'm moving back up—right after I list my house for sale in Atlanta. I want to come home now," she said.

"Virginia's your home?" Mike said.

"It was. I moved when I got divorced. Phoebe's here. My

father. And you're here too," she said.

"Hey everyone, I hate to break up the party, but I need to ask you to leave. Mr. Netherland needs to eat, then I have to give him some pain killers which are going to quiet him down. Doctor's orders. I can stand by and wait a minute or two if you like first," she said. It was Charlotte, Mike's nurse.

"It's ok. We're done right now. Mike, thanks. You're something else—risking your life to help a stranger. I don't know what to say," she said.

"You don't have to say anything. I'm glad to have done what I did. Georgia," he said. She and her sister started out the door, then stopped. Georgia walked back to him and took his left hand.

"Did you mean what you said to me at the Super24 that first time?" she said. Mike smiled.

"You're a nice unit? Yeah, I did," he said.

"I like that part," she said. Mike smiled.

"I'm looking forward to the coffee," she said. She kissed his hand, then walked out with her sister. Their shoes clicked on the hospital floor as they made their way down the hall to leave the building.

"If you decide you don't want him, can I have him?" Phoebe said.

"He's already taken."